Clay Town, 1954

By George T. Lindsey

Order this book online at www.trafford.com
or email orders@trafford.com

Most Trafford titles are also available at major online book retailers.

Note for Librarians: A cataloguing record for this book is available from Library
and Archives Canada at www.collectionscanada.ca/amicus/index-e.html

Printed in Victoria, BC, Canada.

ISBN: 978-1-4269-0089-1 (sc)
ISBN: 978-1-4269-0091-4 (e-book)

*Our mission is to efficiently provide the world's finest, most comprehensive
book publishing service, enabling every author to experience success.
To find out how to publish your book, your way, and have it available
worldwide, visit us online at www.trafford.com*

Trafford rev. 9/14/2009

 www.trafford.com

North America & international
toll-free: 1 888 232 4444 (USA & Canada)
phone: 250 383 6864 ♦ fax: 812 355 4082

TO ADA

Who covers the full page. I love you!

Contents

Prologue

It was in the '50s, before Kerouac's "On The Road", before the loss of a war in Vietnam, before VCRs and Bluetooths, before the black movement, the women's movement, before the Watergate and Contras, before mass immigration of radically diverse cultures, before the buying of America, before the loss of naiveté and innocence.

It was approaching 1954 in Clay Town with a dwindling population of five thousand, composed mainly of English, Irish, and Italian descendants. There were three churches, Catholic, Presbyterian, and Baptist.

Once each year, in the cycle of this midwestern town, the streets and stores were closed for a parade honoring the clay workers from the few remaining sewer pipe plants surrounding the town. This was before the sewer pipe plants vanished to the cheaper labor of the South, or to extinction.

Dividing the town were four ribbons of tracks belonging to the Pennsylvania railroad, known as the Panhandle. This was the midway point between Columbus and Pittsburgh. On the far side of the tracks was the South Side with the backside of houses showing their vexation for the intrusion of the black billowing, iron clad, smoke-driven rattling trains. On the town side, Center Street ran parallel with the tracks supporting a number of bars, night clubs and two houses of ill-repute. The large brick depot sat deserted across from Center Street. It had weathered the soot of fame as the celebrated Clay Town Canteen which offered donuts and coffee to thousands upon thousands of troops headed toward World War Two. This was before the signals were pulled, the railroad sold to a conglomerate, and the tracks wasted.

There were some who graduated from high school and left, never to return, and who remembered it clearly even when yesterday's temperatures and headlines escaped them as so much sawdust on the floor of sawmills to the gods.

From the '50s, memories are resurrected as if walking through the arduous maze again looking for the rainbow that was only a figment of nature.

In those memories the people of Clay Town resemble ants from atop the surrounding foothills of Appalachia.

Dody Blake lugs a suitcase toward the busy Clay Town train depot. He is leaving for boot-camp. His father, The General, stands proud.

Edna Breakers oils her uncle's gun and points it toward a mirror in her bedroom.

Karl Schmidt stands at the window of the mayor's office and stares down idle Grant Street, content for the moment, only for the moment.

Paul Steiner swings his lunch pail as he crosses over the hill separating the Ottoman Plant, one of a half dozen sprawling clay works, surrounding the town. He passes the overgrown Catholic cemetery which looks down on the house-size ovens and three story building. It is the first jungle ruins Paul is to encounter. It will not be his last.

Harry O'Brien carts his half filled mail sack along Third Street cursing at the uplifted slabs and sidewalk cracks.

J.C. Pulton hugs a packaged bottle as he leaves the liquor store minutes after it opened.

Agatha Breakers totes a book from the Clay Town library,

located in City Hall, where she meets every Friday night with the book club. She hates the innovation of television.

Jinny Pin sorts through a handful of envelopes filled with overdue bills and enters her second floor office in the Pin Department Store. She pretends not to see the lone customer looking at the rolls of cloth which will never be sold.

Doctor Rider hauls the black medicine bag to his rusted Plymouth without haste or determination. There will be fights tonight with cuts and broken bones to fix, and they will come to him even though he is a veterinarian.

Alice Golding extracts a drink from the living room bar. She stops at the large bay window overlooking the hills. She sips from the glass and disappears into the bedroom.

Mrs. Flutters waters a wilting plant in her tiny apartment. Her now wrinkled life is spent in wakes for friends.

Jimmy McBridy eyes a 16 gage shotgun behind the glass counter.

Father Cromley picks crab grass from the sidewalk cracks in front of his church.

Mona Ottoman pulls a locked chest from its hiding place inside the dark closet as Clara, her sister, sits immobile engulfed in black.

Mrs. Simpson walks up to the door of the Ottoman mansion which will become her new nursing home.

Dag Mercer hikes at his wrinkled trousers while walking down the railroad tracks where grass pushes its way between dirty cinders. He pulls a tiny hamster from his pocket and places it on his shoulder. The retarded youth is walking on a carousel which never moves except around and around and around. Those he passes, Grover McFadden, Mrs. Grimes, Mr. Wilson, Leo Angelo, The General, Abe Tatter, all are caught on the same revolving carousel. No matter how fast, how far they run in any direction, they cannot escape the carousel's turning, whirling centrifugal force. Dag walks on and stares at the lights and dilapidated structures not wanting to look past the clay horses.

In less than thirty years the whore houses, the beer joints, the pool hall, the night clubs, the integral guts of the town will lay fallow as vacant lots, reminders of what it was like in 1954.

Part I

SUMMER

The Factory

In the '50s the economy was such that sewer pipe was in demand. This paid the keep for a number of Clay Town residents, men with big guts, tough skin, and strong muscles. Some could slug the hell out of the coal miners and railroad section hands over around Cadiz and as far as Mingo Junction. Inside the soot-stained brick building, which resembled a sweat factory of industrialized England, they prepared the wet molded pipe for loading into large-domed brick kilns in the yards outside where it would be baked into sturdy clay pipe guaranteed to last for hundreds of years.

Three men, standing in a whirl of clay dust seeping through cracks in the floor, bent toward their work at a revolving steel table. The large frame of Abe Tatter pulled the worn phallic handle attached to the grotesque hulk of machinery. The machine belched and a wet clay pipe materialized. Jerking the rod, Abe smiled, spit, and awaited the next gray clay defecation. The soft pipe hung for a moment as if suspended by the very will of Abe then was caught in the small bony hands of Johnny Diker ending on the revolving machine where they rotated like church candles.

Gilley Tarman, sitting perched on a high wooden stool, trimmed each pipe as they circled in front of him. Tarman trimmed the pipe with a small steel knife looking much like an acolyte extinguishing candles with devout and gentle homage.

Suddenly the machine stopped and the stiff, dust-streaked face of Abe Tatter became tighter. His skin furrowed and became ripples of anger.

"Where's Pulton?"

Both Johnny Diker and Gilley Tarman flinched and looked toward the flatbed truck half loaded with wet pipe standing unattended in front of the revolving table.

"Don't know," Gilley said easing his steel knife.

"Maybe he went to the pee pee," Johnny Diker said starting to load the pipe onto the truck to cover for the missing workman.

"He knows better'n that!" Abe shouted as his wrath traveled through the low, dust filled room shaking with the pounding steel presses. Abe relaxed his command on the maker. "He knows better'n that!" The press stopped. "How can we make pipe when them floormen don't cooperate!"

The two subordinates stretched themselves and looked around. Johnny lighted a cigarette and blew the white smoke toward the jaw of the machine.

"Heathen!" Abe shouted. "Smokin' and cussin'! You young devils are all heathens! Hear me, Diker?"

Johnny blew another cloud of smoke in response.

"Godless, inconsiderate heathens, that's what you'ens are!" Abe shouted again, forgetting the maker and the missing floorman as he turned his wide round eyes toward Johnny Diker.

"Call yourselves Catholics and Methodists and Presbyterians! You hide behind them names, I say! Them religions just let you carry on your heathen practices so you can call yourselves them to make people believe you're half good!"

Gilley Tarman climbed once more onto his wooden acolyte stool and smiled. He had listened to the wrath of Abe Tatter for twelve years and the sermon had never changed.

"Hey Abe! Your knees sore this morning from all that praying?" Gilley asked, bored with the monotonous clay candles circling around him.

Abe bent over the lower workings of the machine and greased it by sticking his hand into a can beside him then rubbing it on the steel rod. The men were no longer present to Abe's consciousness. He had spent his anger.

"Here comes Dag Mercer!" Johnny whispered to Gilley. "Bet he's lookin' for a job like he always does around Clay Day."

"You know what to do, huh?" Gilley asked squirming on his seat.

"Sure. Sure."

Dag Mercer, sniffing the dust, propelled his awkward body toward the large clay press. His thoughts, like the jerky movements of his body, struggled to find expression through a thick tongue. He stumbled against a dry pipe resting near the elevator. The cracked clay pipe fell to the wooden floor. Dag jumped when the pipe shattered into pieces. He stopped and stooped trying to piece them together. When his effort failed he straightened and began the uncontrolled walk toward the press. His frayed cloth jacket had been quickly covered with gray dust which seemed to please Dag. The powder hid the letter C on his red ball cap.

"Har. You fellas know where boss is?"

"Lookin' for a job, Dag?" Johnny asked keeping a straight face.

"Har. Sure is." Dag answered with a grin. "No more errands in town. Gonna make livin' here."

"But don't you work at the funeral place?" Tarman asked innocently behind a giggle.

"Nope. Just help Mr. McBridy out now'n then. Don't get paid hardly nothing."

"Ya mean he don't pay you?"

"Har. Sure, he give me some, but 'tain't steady. Where's boss? I see him and get real job."

Johnny looked at Gilley Tarman who sat high on the stool then he turned to Dag. "You got to see Mr. Pulton. He's around somewheres."

"Har. He boss?"

"Sure. He does the hiring."

"What's going on there?" Abe sternly asked as he stopped greasing the press. "Who's leg you pullin'?"

"Now Abe, let's tell Dag where he can find the boss," Johnny said making a sign for Abe to go along with the joke. Abe became silent and concerned himself with the rod as if it were a divine instrument of God.

"Now Dag, you got to find Mister Pulton 'cause he does the hiring. You go up and call him boss, real nice like, and I think he'll give you a job."

"Har. Mister Pulton. I go find 'im."

"Hey Dag! Ready for this year's parade?" Gilley asked from his security atop the stool.

"Gonna lead parade 'gain?" Johnny asked breaking out in laughter.

"Always lead parade. Mayor give me this for leading parade," Dag answered opening his jacket and displaying a whistle dangling by a string around his neck. Before the men could speak, Dag blew it loudly.

"Get him out of here!" Abe shouted over the shrill sound. Dag, tripping on his heels, ran off into the dim of clay dust.

"Why did you send him to that wino?" Abe asked resuming his post with dignity becoming a cutter. "Pulton can't keep up his own job without joking with that poor stupid fool."

"Now Abe, it's just a little fun we's havin'. Old Pulton can really put on the act." Johnny said wiping his hands in anticipation to the forthcoming event.

"Here he comes, and Dag ain't seen 'im yet. Better hurry up, Pulton!" Johnny shouted turning toward the missing truckman.

The plump stomach of J. C. Pulton, supported in a mystical airship fashion, advanced toward them followed by his working stubs of feet and topped by two beady bloodshot eyes and a large red nose.

"Where the devil you been, heathen?" Abe asked starting up the clay press as if God had been insulted by the disappearance of the floorman.

"Shut up ya old holy roller!" Pulton said before lifting the pipe onto his flatbed truck. "I thought it was high time for a break and you holy rollers don't let a decent man stop for no peace on earth."

Abe's thick forehead became red. He hated the wino and was sensitive to any remark Pulton voiced. Pulton, unaware of the pressman's mood, continued talking while lifting the pipe destined for stacking, like doomed souls, in the domed ovens outside.

"Someday I'm gonna knock you on your 'ass and make you roll in this here dust. That'll give you a god all right!"

"You been drinking again, heathen!" Abe roared. "You been down in the dry bin where you hide your bottle and you been fillin' your gut with rotten wine! I'm going to have you fired one of these days because we can't tolerate a man who don't believe in his Maker and 'cause you drink on company time!"

"Why don't ya get on your knees and pray for me!" Pulton said knowing he could not openly deny he had been drinking.

"I'll pray! I'll pray, you heathen! I'll drag you through hell itself after this morning's over! Hear me! After this morning you see me in the woods back of the clay bin!" Abe shouted, then, calmed by the sudden burst of anger, jerked the steel rod into place as a wet clay pipe slid from the machine. His movement ended further talk.

Tarman, watching the scene atop his wooden stool, saw Dag

enter the dusty room. Dag's here again, Pulton. He's coming to you to git a job. We told 'im, like last year, didn't we Johnny?"

No sooner had Tarman spoke than Dag was standing before them.

"Har. Can't find Mister Pulton for nothing. Been all over."

"Why son, you ain't looked hard 'nuff or far enough. That's me. J.C. Pulton."

"You boss?"

"I'm Pulton."

"Well, can I have a job they talk 'bout, har, Mister boss? Can I have it?"

"Ever work at a clay works?"

"Har. Run errands for the one up the way." Dag exclaimed pointing toward the front of the building.

"Ever handle pipe?"

Dag shook his head.

"Here. You just put a couple of these on the truck," Pulton said, moved aside, and motioned Dag to take his place between the truck and the circling platform holding the newly ejected pipe. Dag squeezed the first pipe attempting to lift it, but the soft clay was crushed between his hands.

"No, no, son. That's not the spirit. Them pipe's alive. You got to handle 'em like children."

"Har, alive?"

"Yep. They're alive all right. Hey Tar, don't your kids eat 'cause them pipe's alive, just don't they?"

"Sure do Mister Pulton," the perched acolyte replied.

Abe had been pulling and jerking the rod methodically trying not to become involved. Each time his eyes raised they met Pulton's gaze. Finally Abe forgot the rod's movements, handling it with practice and keeping his stare on the heathen who was giving Dag instructions.

"Ya see, lad, them pipe's our blood. The dust gets inside us and that's what makes us clay men."

The workers sanctioned the soliloquy with applause.

"Now, if you can't handle them pipe, you're no son of the sons of clay workers, so handle 'em gently."

Dag crushed another soft pipe between his hands but succeeded in his next attempt. The pipe's bottom was flattened by impact with the truck bed.

"That's good, lad. Ya showed your worth. Now you're on your way ta becoming a clay man."

"Har. I work then?"

"Sure, but first ya got to prove your judgment. Now you run along to kiln number five and ask Joe out there to give you a sky bar so's we can put this here truck in the attic. Sky bar. Got that?"

"Har! Sky bar. I get it soon," Dag shouted disappearing into the dust leaving Pulton staring into the eyes of Abe. The men laughed soundly with the exit of Dag. They congratulated Pulton for his showmanship and wit, but the rotund man disregarded their cheers.

"Tar an' tendation," Pulton remarked pushing the crushed pipe aside. "It's hard makin' life agreeable to you fellows when there's fake ministers showin' their ugly faces."

The press stopped for the second time and Abe walked toward the truckman.

"You been drinking, you wino, or I'd clean knock your head off!"

"Wino?" Pulton spit on Abe's heavy leather shoes. "A Goddamn fat-headed bastard like you who knocked up his woman 'fore marryin' her then turning and hiding behind religion don't need to call nobody names!"

Abe took Pulton's neck between his large muscular hands and pushed the fat man over the truck flattening the soft wet pipe. Johnny and Gilley quickly grabbed Abe by the arms. Both talked softly.

"He didn't mean no harm. We all kid, Abe. Leave 'im alone. You know he's not well when he's been drinkin' all night. It'll pass."

Abe shook both men off with a sudden quiver and walked back to the steel rod. "I had 'nuff of that pot-bellied whore-hound," Pulton said pulling himself upright and brushing his tattered clothes. "I'll see him in the woods."

The break siren ended any expletives and the two angry men went their separate ways to sip coffee. Johnny and Tarman slipped their thermos bottles off the shelf and returned to the table which was quiet in the break stillness. They sat and poured liquid into dusty cups.

"He'll kill old Pulton," Johnny said taking a sip.

"Naw. Pulton won't be at work after the break. He's hanging one on and he'll head for the Westway and get himself a bottle of wine. That'll cool both of 'em off."

"Someday Abe's gonna kill 'im. I tell you," Johnny answered pouring coffee. Suddenly Dag was standing in front of them his hands thrust in his Levis.

"No sky bar nowheres. I look all over."   The two men laughed.

"Well Dag," Tarman spoke between sips. "That don't lay none too good with Mister Pulton. He ain't gonna hire no one who can't find a important piece of machinery like a sky bar."

"I work hard for money," Dag said taking off his hat and dusting it. He felt like crying.

"Sorry Dag. You come back some other time. Mister Pulton said he wouldn't hire you 'less you came back with the sky bar."

Dag disappeared into the dust. He emerged onto the hot sun of summer and sat on the fire escape overlooking the workers at their break, sitting idly between burning kilns, drinking coffee, talking, being happy.

"Har!" Dag said aloud to himself. "I get sky bar. Buy it in town and bring it to Mister Pulton."

His mood turned happy. The noonday sun was bright on his face and he still had the hope of a job. Dag almost fell down the steel fire escape rushing to buy the imaginary sky bar. Again this year, he would lead the Clay Parade. People along the sidewalk would recognize him in the Uncle Sam suit and he would hold Mousie, his pet hamster, for them to see. They would smile and laugh, but Dag was especially happy since this year he would be a real clay worker and could take pride in the festivities.

The hills of Clay Town began their ascent behind the giant brick building. Two men struggled for control at the edge of the trees. "Heathen! Heathen! Heathen!" Abe Tatter shouted again and again as he hit Pulton. "God won't have no mercy on thee and neither will I, being His disciple!"

Pulton, held tightly against a tree by Abe's strength, breathed blood. "Whore-hound, whore-hound," he whispered with his tongue hanging against his lower teeth. "Whore-hound , whore-hound."

Smack came the knuckles against the fatty tissue of Pulton's cheek. Smack, the fist smashed against the hard bone of his forehead. Buff, Pulton gasped as the fist found his stomach sending the air through the blood of his mouth.

"Heathen! Heathen! You deserve death and damnation!"

Abe was not without bruise marks from Pulton's thrusts. He could not see from his swollen left eye, nor could he move his left shoulder where Pulton's cudgel had found its mark. Abe, exhausted from hitting the fat body, relaxed his hold and Pulton immediately paid him a cuff across the nose which sent tears mingling with sweat to Abe's eyes. He was down and Pulton, taking advantage of the prone position, kicked out furiously.

He aimed at the groin and found it soft and penetrable. Then Pulton again held the heavy branch and was beating Abe's face and stomach.

The McBridy ambulance, carrying Abe on the cot and Pulton across a make-shift stretcher, passed Dag as it screamed toward town. Dag awkwardly ran a few steps after the siren then slowed again. He tried to sing because he was happy but the words became confused in his mind.

"Oh what a beautiful morning, Oh what a beautiful day. Everything's turning out, turning out, turning out... okay."

Storm Cloud

The Pin Department Store sat across from City Hall on Grant Street. The large two story structure housed items purchased for sale in another time: bolts of cloth, sewing machines, outdated trinkets, calico dresses, overalls, cotton blankets.

The high ceiling was embossed tin, hinting of a style used in the twenties. There was a pneumatic tube which shot bills and messages from the upstairs office to the counters below. All was unused and unwanted in 1953.

Jinny Pin leaned out the office window and allowed the breeze to drift swiftly through her hair. The rushing stimulation seemed to vibrate each strand. Jinny was delighted. Two stories below, or was it a hundred, she watched as the summer wind moved through the trees, the bushes, the wasted newspapers cluttering the sidewalk. Jinny thought hard about a written history of triviality in news print discarded by someone below who had no further use for symbols of printed ink, all below, caught in the unperceiving cache of the wrestling intruding wind.

Filled with spastic delight she welcomed the dismal approaching clouds of darkness which threatened rain. The gray clouds matched the store below. Dark, foreboding, unwanted.

Come. Come! The sun, the moon, the revolving earth. Come, come! My body awaits you. Come! I am ready, she thought. I am no longer a youth, no longer a maiden, a high school girl with dreams of love and gentleness. I am ready! Before it's too late!

Suddenly, unaware of her surroundings, her face jerked away from the open window. Embarrassment blanketed her freedom. "This is no way to act." There was no one in the office but she spoke aloud.

"My God! It's absurd! The cool rain, water. Me, a part of it?"

She quickly returned to her desk, gathered three pencils hurriedly and walked to the opposite side of the office. She surveyed her desk while mechanically turning the sharpener. Gray, everything somber gray, she thought, because of the approaching storm, because of this dead store, gray, lifeless. The office remained silent, only the stimulating wind wrestled the thick stack of yellow papers on the old desk. It's penetrating the grayness and shuffling emptiness, she thought. Before Jinny returned to the desk, the grayness had become almost black. The storm was approaching rapidly. The two sales girls had departed early to ready themselves for the evening.

Friday, Jinny thought, day of reckoning. The sensation again churned her stomach with excitement as a puff of air climbed her thighs. She sat down and crossed her long slim legs. She unconsciously tugged at her skirt.

The bell attached to the front door announced a customer.

"The storm is almost here," she said quietly to herself and left the office to wait on the customer.

Dag Mercer leaned against the thick glass show case hiding the long rows of cloth beneath. Not finding a sky bar, he slipped to the floor, and reached into his Levis pulling out a black scouting knife. Dag opened the blades and stuck the large end in the floor. The shinny blade sparkled in the glass reflection. He placed his index finger beneath the knife and pulled upward. The knife jumped into the air and bounced against the glass counter.

13

"Har! Har!" Dag uttered in fright, quickly shutting the blades into the holder and slipping it again to the depth of his pocket.

"Har! Har," he mumbled looking around the dark, quiet department store. The high ceilings could not be seen, and Dag crawled to the end of the glass counter peeking quickly around it.

"Where are thee, Dagburt? Show thyself!"

"Har, har, here, Miss Pin. Cleaning floor."

Miss Pin stood high and thin above Dag, even with her diminutive height of five feet three inches, staring from behind pinched nose glasses. She played with a bare ring finger. Her cotton dress swished around her ankles. "Be quick, Dagburt. What are thee about?"

"Cleaning floor. I only clean floor," Dag said taking out his red bandanna.

"Thee know, Dagburt. Thee mus'n't wash during working hours."

"I no warsh 'em, just clean," Dag said as he scrambled to his feet and shook the bandanna. "Errand, Miss Pin? Har, want I go after cigars?"

"Hush Dagburt. Do not breathe that!"

"Har, har, no Miss Pin. Do you got Sky Bar?"

"What is a Sky Bar?" Jinny asked innocently.

"Need it at Ottoman plant. Sent me looking. Need job."

"Take thyself to the front office upstairs and sweep there, Dagburt. It will earn thee a dollar."

"Got to find Sky Bar," Dag said as he sank to the floor and pulled out his scout knife. "Har, Miss Pin. You ever play jackknife?"

(Glide over the discarded newspaper, condoms, cigar butts, wet, cool.)

"No. I've watched though, in grade school."

(The machine vibrates onward until subdued by rust.)

"Mr. McBridy taught me when we was waiting for the funeral to git over. Gave me this." Dag felt his gift.

(Stick it in me! Let me die!) "It's pretty. Put it away, Dag."

"Har, I learned good."

"Show me."

"Here?"

"Yes, here." Jinny said as she sank down beside the glass case and pointed to the floor. Her silk clad knees slipped from the cotton dress. The nylons squeezed until red spots appeared at her knees. "Here. Show me." Dag knelt down beside her.

(Stick it in me!)

"It's fun," Dag said as he flipped the knife and it jumped, hitting the case and bounced onto Jinny's lap. He reached for the knife and felt his hand being squeezed as she brought her legs tightly together. She pressed the hand with all the strength in her thighs and then let it move quickly back to Dag.

(What am I doing? Stick me!)

"That's dangerous, Dag. Very dangerous."

"Mr. McBridy said I must watch careful."

"Yes, you must watch carefully, Dag."

(Stick it! Stick it!)

"Har, Miss Pin?"

"There's a storm coming. Ever see the streets during a terrible storm?"

"Har, yep, Miss Pin. Walked 'em lots, even when that tornado came through a few years back an' took off the church roof."

"Do you ever become lonely, Dag?"

"Not with jackknife."

"And without your knife?"

Dag flipped the knife watching it fall on the long point.

"Har, har, a good'un."

"Yes it is, but what's the use being here. No one ever comes. Mother keeps the store for her pleasure on Daddy's pension."

"I knew Mr. Pin," Dag said awakening to the mention of his former friend. "He got run over by train, har."

"He was drunk."

"Mr. McBridy said he was all messed up."

"She works all day long cleaning shelves, straightening the goods, and no one ever comes to buy. Why Dag? Why must I stay here?"

"I got keep knife oiled or it'll rust."

(Stick! Stick! Stick!)

"Why in God's name must I die here?"

"Soft wood is good to stick knife in."

No sooner had Dag spoken then the knife fell to the floor and the long blade snapped. He seized the broken piece and forgot the rest. Dag bounced to his feet. "It broke! Broke!"

"Please go!" Jinny said with anger biting her tongue. "You and your knives! Men and their childish wants. Mother is right to shut herself away! Keep the world out! Go find your Sky Bar."

Dag stooped, picked up the broken knife blade and left the store. There were tears in his eyes.

(It in me! It in me!)

Jinny was at the window and the rain came. Hugging her shoulders, Jinny stared into the rain but the drops did not touch her. Without her sweater, she turned and ran to the front door, her heels echoing off the high walls.

"What art you doing? I didn't know you were still here?" her mother shouted.

She ran and left her mother's voice far behind. Beyond the door was the sweetness of the rain mounting. Jinny scurried across Grant Street. She felt the rain's familiar beat as it touched her skin with kisses of passion, each drop tantalizing her inner need. She whirled and opened her mouth allowing the wetness to penetrate her orifice. She tried to look directly into the rain but it stung her eyes. Was she crying or did rain drops replace the salty aftermath of despair.

The sudden summer's shower shrieked fury through a moment's ejaculation and scuttled once again over the hills. She felt the steam bath effect of the storm as she slowly walked. Books again tonight, wild words of freedom in Balzac, Whitman — stick, store, books, work, work, crazy opium bliss in repression. The town opened its doors and she began to slow her pace walking north to nowhere in particular.

Naked Cross

The size eight and a half shoes of Jimmy McBridy sank into the soft sponge clay of the hill. He stood below a summer's quarter moon surveying the distant yellow lights of Clay Town, squinting across the dripping valley on the north slope of the hill from where he had started to climb. Standing on the peak of the highest hill, Jimmy watched the tiny lights sparkle through the weeds. He felt the clammy clay sink beneath him, and he knew it was dirty and yellow. Leaving the path, which wiggled upward through pines and elms, he entered a large vacant clearing covered with crab grass and weeds. Jimmy squeezed a pimple on his chin awaiting the signal.

The topography of the hills fascinated Jimmy. The hills behind his home had offered hot days of hiking over the slopes, made by the last of the great glaciers. Now, on a Friday evening, he waited for Dag to call. Looking in every direction, Jimmy felt the hot summer breeze and pulled the black Dacron coat collar against his neck. Dag had warned him to wear dark clothes.

Jimmy's fair complexion hid behind the blackness of the clothes.

"Har, Jimmy, Here." Dag was whispering at the southern edge of the clearing where his recent urination steamed from the weeds.

"Har, har, this way. Down here apiece. You see 'em, you see 'em."

"Okay, okay," Jimmy moved toward Dag rejoining the slumped companion near a patch of thick pine trees. Dag waited then climbed down the slope. Jimmy, small and agile, followed him into the woods below and both boys, half running, half stumbling, passed through the underbrush with the agility of Indians. Dag grabbed Jimmy's jacket before they had paced a hundred yards. Jimmy felt the tug and halted; at once torch light encircled the trees. Jimmy, unaware, had almost run head long into a lighted clearing. He could recognize that the reddish glow was originating from fire, but he could not see a flame, only a dim, steady light causing dark shadows to move in the trees. Then Dag knelt and Jimmy fell breathlessly beside him.

"Har, we stay here. Sometime they go to woods. You keep tight and watch."

"Garsh, sure," Jimmy answered in a whisper lower than his companion's. Black pine trees sprouted like splintery totem poles above him.

"Har, they there!" Dag exclaimed. "See 'em good. See, I here before."

Jimmy could not answer. His bladder became full and his breath came between gulps as though he were again on the top of the hill with his chest hot and pounding. Men, supporting white robes, seemed to dance into the clearing. They resembled Catholic priests, Jimmy thought, thinking about the priests at mass with their long gowns. Jimmy recovered from a sudden spasm of chill and tapped Dag on the shoulder.

"Why do they wear hoods, huh, Dag?" Dag crawled another foot closer to the clearing as if to inspect the hoods. He hid himself behind a clump of rag weed; Jimmy followed hesitating until the furrowed ground became a circle in front of him enclosed by tree shadows. The light shot into the sky from a four foot flaming cross stuck in the soft earth. The bright flames lighted the entire clearing. He was frightened of the light.

"Why they got to burn a cross?" He again whispered to Dag.

"Har, har, that cross mean they mad."

"Then why do they got to meet way out here? And why they got to cover their heads?"

"Don't know," Dag answered. "Been here before. Still don't know."

A hundred questions entered Jimmy's thoughts, but Dag was quiet beside him. Earlier in the evening the questions could have been asked — there was time when Jimmy wheeled his bicycle along Whitham road outside Clay Town, and Dag sat atop the handlebars, but now Dag was silent and Jimmy was scared. He wanted to ask Dag why a man wearing khakis was pulled to the cross by two men dressed in white robes and hoods. Loud shouting voices penetrated the stillness around them. Jimmy kept the fear to himself.

The leader, a scarecrow in white, stood in front of the cross. The struggling man was forced to his knees as if to pay tribute to the cross and leader. The shouts faded as the highness extended his arms and spoke.

"Crackers, you've been a good member of this here organization, but God Almighty, now your granddaddy be ashamed of you. We always got on with you and your pa in the past. You helped us out when them niggers tried to settle here, but now, you got to take action 'gain." The high priest turned toward the flaming cross and pointed his finger.

The kneeling man, hands tied tightly behind him, lowered his head. Shadows danced around his face, creating sharp-edged points. Between the red, black, and yellow glare, Jimmy thought the man's skin was melting; sweat dripped from his nose. Crackers' chest appeared as big as a mountain, his biceps knotted into lumps resembling cannon balls, and the muscles of his thighs were long, taunt ridges tight against the khaki trousers. Jimmy knew Crackers, but he did not like the electric company worker. Only last week Crackers had visited the McBridy Funeral Home, and Jimmy's father, Bud McBridy, told Mrs. McBridy at the dinner table that Crackers was white trash. Jimmy remembered his father saying that Crackers was also a trouble maker and that he, Crackers, worked for a radical group in the town, claiming affiliation with the Klu Klux Klan, calling themselves the democratic crusaders. The word Klu Klux Klan struck fear into Jimmy. The title was ugly and the white robes against the black night were ugly. Jimmy knew Crackers and the robed men would kill him if discovered; hadn't they killed a black man once — that was gossiped by everyone, even if the killing had occurred before Jimmy was old enough to remember. He had taken his father's warning and avoided meeting Crackers on the street. But the youth felt compassion toward the sweating man. A dream? Jimmy was not asleep. He felt the prick of pine needles. Jimmy turned his gaze from the suffering man and counted the priests forming a semi-circle around the flaming cross. Three, five, ten, fifteen robes, fifteen counting the high priest. The men, silently staring at Crackers, faced uphill. Their eyes gazed hypnotically at the cross. Jimmy felt the men watch. He turned to Dag, but the retard was stroking his pet hamster, Mousie, which he had taken from deep inside his jacket pocket, unconcerned with the flames of the cross. It was enough to Dag that he had led Jimmy to the promised meeting, and now he waited patiently until Jimmy wanted to go, waited in the bushes until he could collect the promised award.

"You got to change your mind," the high priest continued. "Them niggers over at the Royal plant need a scaring. No rough stuff, you just scare up that Templeton family like we told ya."

"By damn, I won't change my mind," the kneeling man raised his head. "We've been through this mess before. I say let 'em come in. You guys're crazy."

The leader leaned swiftly forward and struck Crackers, the

sound of bone meeting flesh echoed across the clearing. The high priest examined his hands, rubbed them against his robe, then stepped hastily back.

"Sorry Crackers. I don't want dirty play, but Christ, we been paying you these years to keep 'em and foreigners out. Now you get snobby with us. It ain't fair. Can't you see, them people coming in will ruin our women and make future kids unclean."

"No, I don't see no how." Crackers began to cry.

"Come on, Crackers," a robe spoke. "We got rid of 'em niggers once, didn't we? You weren't so Goddamn holy 'bout 'em then."

The kneeling man twisted toward the crowd behind him. "That was then. I don't want none of your Goddamn organization now. I changed. I changed and I don't want no more so leave me alone."

"We know all 'bout you," another gown shouted. "We seen you sneaking 'round with 'er. You ain't gonna hurt your girlfriend, are you?"

"That's right, Crackers," the high priest turned Crackers again toward the cross. "Bill followed you them last couple Friday nights to the meeting place with her"

"Jesus Christ, all we did was talk!" Crackers exclaimed.

"No matter. You was with 'er. Now we don't mind you going 'gainst the organization so much, but taking up with 'er, well, that's being downright dirt. It's white trash like you that brings 'em to nice towns. If this was the city, you could get away with making love, but this is Clay Town and we're gonna make sure you don't forget."

"I tell you, it's not so." Crackers' face became white against the red flames, bathed in sweat. "We just met and talked. She's nice, she's smart. We talked 'bout things 'round the world. She was gonna teach me to speak French, and, and, she's pretty."

"Pretty, huh? Sure 'nuff," the high priest walked close to

Crackers and his spit splashed into Crackers' face as though the leader was baptizing the man with words.

"Next you'll have 'er on the ground and give 'er a baby, then the baby'll grow up and rape my little girl, and we'll have the blood in my family. Isn't that right, brothers?" They cheered the words.

"That's not so," Crackers shouted, but the high priest slapped him.

"Let's be done with 'im!" Shouted another robe. "He's with 'em!"

"You're right, Sam. He's got to be our example. Like Jim Watson was. It sent them niggers running!"

Jimmy wiggled back, tapped Dag's heel and motioned for him to follow. Dag, playing with the furry animal, at first did not understand. He had forgotten about the voices. Now he was forced back to the words and he replaced Mousie, quietly following Jimmy. When they reached the clearing at the top of the hill, both boys were breathing hard.

"Har, bet you no see nothing like that? Give it me, now, har, you promise."

Jimmy wanted to run, but Dag was standing in front of him. He reached into the dacron jacket and felt the Jack-knife.

"You promise not to tell nobody 'bout bringin' me here?"

"I no tell. Give it me."

Jimmy handed Dag the scout knife he had promised. Shouts of men, behind, below, met them out of the thickness of the trees.

"Let's go Dag." But Dag was on his knees, groping for the knife, flipping it.

"You'll have time to play later!" Dag arose reluctantly.

"Your Daddy taught me good to play but broke knife in wood. Ground's best for to flip. Har, I no break this 'un."

Jimmy pulled Dag along the path hurrying back toward the squinting lights of Clay Town.

"Don't you tell nobody 'bout this," Jimmy repeated for the third time. "If anybody hears we'll be in trouble and they'll take your knife away."

Dag nodded and gripped the knife tightly. They parted in silence.

Walking to the McBridy Funeral Home, Jimmy felt sadness for Crackers. He did not know why, even if his father had called Crackers white trash, even if they said he had killed. Jimmy began to feel close to the man tied on the hill. Crackers had always spoken on the street, now Jimmy wished he had returned Crackers' greetings. Jimmy, afraid of his trip, could not report the meeting and what he had witnessed. He began to doubt his own senses — the meeting in the woods was not real — it was easy to forget. He entered the Funeral Parlor where Larry, his father, and mother were entertaining guests. Jimmy entered the somber chamber and forgot the woods.

Shirley Templeton was a Negro by birth, and she felt pride for her race. But Shirley had not found a man to understand her depth. They wanted her body. She wanted their intellects. She came to Clay Town because her parents settled there. No reason was necessary. It was a town and a life. Shirley offered no reason.

She knew she had a soul, but her thoughts, complex as they seemed to Crackers, were simple. She reached out each morning and brought in beauty with each tiny fist.

Shirley was a secretary at the Clay Town Electric Company, and she filled her hands with the beauty of work. She was liked by the employees, but she was a Negro, and while she gave them beauty, they held her grace at social lengths as if to say, we like you, we like your work, but you are Shirley Templeton, born a Negro.

Summer reminded Shirley of the South, not because she was born in that far away country, not because she admired cotton fields, not because the South's heat was in her blood, and she knew it would be years, centuries, eons, before the blood adjusted to the cold of the North. She liked the summer more than the winter, and she liked Friday evenings more than the whole week. It was on Friday evenings she talked with Crackers when they met at Blacksmith Pond, behind the weekend skirts of the town and night.

Shirley did not love Crackers. She was certain that Crackers did not desire her. She knew love to be sweat, chase, conquer, regret, but her meetings with Crackers were only release without the shame, and she looked forward to Fridays with curbed happiness and beauty, knowing only that they were wrong, in the eyes of the town's people, but feeling pleasure all the same. Shirley rocked in the wicker chair on the dilapidated porch watching blackness of night approach the low, shabby roofs around her, thinking of summer and playing with a charm hanging between her full breasts, crossing and uncrossing her legs nervously, waiting and watching. She prayed unaware that she prayed, and the charm, with a cross projecting from the silver surface, became wet from the perspiration of Shirley's hand. Soon she rose and slipped quietly to the back of the house, found the creek, and followed its wiggles until, at last, she came to Blacksmith Pond in the northern section of Clay Town.

Shirley sat on the dry ground, encircled with weeds and wondered what had happened to Crackers. He had never been late in the many Fridays they had met. Then she thought about the Fridays. How many? Ten, twenty, a hundred, million, and her body became restless for love. She must stop coming. Each Friday night she promised herself, and each following Friday she sat with him. The emptiness was filling with restless blood and soon he would demand flesh. She cried but stopped when the sounds of a pick-up truck approached. Quickly, Shirley slipped into the water and walked to the opposite bank. From her position against weeds, she saw the robes, smeared with black, and she saw what they had done to Crackers, her confessor. He protested as they pulled him from the truck; he groaned when they pulled his tarred body toward the creek.

Shirley wanted to scream, but the voices frightened her. They threw Crackers onto the ground and began searching the surrounding area for her. She heard the men talking.

"She left, huh Sam?"

"Guess she couldn't wait for her lover. Hear that, Crackers, she left you to take it all alone. Now I don't call that love."

Crackers tried to speak but his mouth was filled with pain.

"You just lay here and groan and think, huh Crackers."

The robes left and Shirley waited fifteen minutes before she crossed the creek. She sobbed, hearing the groans from Crackers, but her sobs were filled with fear. She reached the mass of crawling tar and feathers. Shirley kissed his tar blackened lips and eyes. The touch of him made her aware that now, with the tenderness of love and compassion, she had killed something inside her. Crackers tried to struggle away from her, but Shirley, with unashamed emotion, gathered his stinking body close and cried. She became covered with reeking tar, and the feathers irritated her skin. She held him close.

Later, when she realized his agony, Shirley helped Crackers along the creek route to her house where she gently wiped away the tar. It was near midnight when they reached her section of town, and the tar, drying on her skin, made her shiver with coldness.

When Crackers recovered from the sores caused by the hot tar, he never thanked Shirley. Each Friday night he went out and got drunk. The men passed him on the street and he feared them.

Shirley, more and more, stayed in her section after work, and Crackers quit the electric company, taking a job with sewer plant number two. The Friday following the meeting in the woods, he tore up his organization card. A change came over Crackers, and he got married. On the same evening, when Crackers tore up his card, Shirley threw the charm into the creek and sent an application to a radical Negro group, based in Washington, D.C.

Heat

"Got ya!"

"You don't!" Edna Breakers tried to cover the checkerboard with her arms but only succeeded in knocking two round checker pieces onto the floor. At the same time the young girl released a stream of giggles.

"Now Edna, I got ya, so don't be trying to cheat." Gumpy Breakers picked up the oil stained revolver and pointed it at Edna.

"I got ya now." Edna shrieked then broke into laughter.

"You don't play fair a'tal."

Gumpy Breakers replaced the gun on the table and bent with much labor to pick up the two fallen pieces.

"Okay Gumpy, you win this one, but I'll get you the next."

Gumpy smiled and red blotches came to his face as he straightened.

"You haven't beat me in a month of Fridays."

"I need practice."

"That why you come here every Friday instead of going out with kids?"

"I need protection and what better place to get it then here?"

They both laughed. Gumpy slid into his official policeman's jacket and began to button it carefully. The third button was missing and Gumpy looked alarmingly at the hanging thread.

"Better have mom fix it for me."

"I can sew it."

"Naw, mom wouldn't like that. Your grandmother's been sewing my uniforms for ten years, and no good-looking dame is going to take her place, she says. Even if it's my sister's kid." Again they laughed.

"Can I ride with you to check the bars tonight?" Edna did not want to leave. She fingered each checker piece before placing it in the worn blue box.

"You know better'n that."

"But you never go in. You just ride around, and I could keep you company."

"That's too late for a youngster like you."

"Gumpy, I graduate this year and I'm going to be working in the bank full time," Edna said with finality, asserting her age.

Gumpy Breakers puffed on his pipe to start it. The resulting clouds hid his round face. He studied Edna for a moment through whiteness then opened the drawer in the counter.

"I got something for ya." He pulled out a magazine and handed it to Edna. The girl forgot her desires to ride in the police car.

"A detective book!"

"Now don't go be telling mom or sis I gave it to you. You just hide it so they won't go getting mad. You know how they feel 'bout crime and sin."

"I will, I will!" Edna was interrupted by the dull buzz of the telephone.

Gumpy Breakers labored to his desk and answered it. "Chief of Police?" He paused and smiled at Edna. "What?" He looked at the desk.

"Yeah." Then he was listening.

Edna felt the yellow of the small office surround her. The blackness of Friday night lay beyond the elongated window, and she could smell the heat of the street through the openings of windows. The yellow, from the overhead bulb, seemed to flicker and move across the room, rippling her black skirt a clay yellow, and her brown, long sleeved blouse, seemed muddy. Then the uniform stood above her and it too was clay yellow.

"You run along."

"Who was it?"

"Business."

Edna knew something had happened since her mother's brother, Gumpy, would never talk about serious police matters.

"Did someone get killed?"

"Nothing serious. Now run along. I got to go."

Edna shoved the checker set into the lower left hand drawer and walked toward the glass door carrying the magazine.

"Someday I'm going to be a police woman."

Gumpy Breakers was loading the revolver when he looked up. "You'd be a good'un."

Edna closed the door and heard her flat heels make hollow sounds through the city hall. The corridor was the same yellow as Gumpy's office, but inside the glass doors which Edna passed, there was darkness. She stopped in front of the library door on the main floor of the city hall, but a yellow shade covered it from inside. She stepped through large front doors leading onto Grant Street and felt the heavy heat.

She remembered how much Gumpy had sweated this summer in his office and while at home. She thought how uncomfortable it must be for him to be so heavy. They'll try to get him out of office now that he's almost fifty, she thought, walking down Grant Street toward the Breakers' home, and he can't get around like when he was young, but he knows his job.

"Where are they?" Gumpy asked from inside the parked police car.

"Inside," Harry O'Brien pointed toward the small, one story house lost in the dark alley. "Like I told you over the phone, they're crazy. Got the place barricaded and just won't come out."

"Been drinkin', huh?"

"Yeah. Shot the bartender down at the Silver Hat. We knew they'd run here 'cause this is Shaparo's place."

"He's a bad'un, but not too bad." Gumpy swam in sweat. He wanted to slide from the hot seat of the police cruiser, but the effort seemed too complex at the moment. Instead, he shifted in the seat.

"Who else is mixed up in it?"

"Billy Pango and Sam Degrade, the three of 'em tried to hold up the place, shot the bartender and ran out. Their car wouldn't start so's they headed here." Harry hurried on. "We got guns, Gumpy, so you just tell us what to do? We can shoot at 'em from here."

"No need of them guns. When you know Shaparo as well as I do, there ain't no need for guns."

"But they killed someone this time!"

"No matter. I know'd him since he was a little fart working at plant number four. He's all breeze." The Chief of Police threw his weight against the car door and stepped into the night. The sweat, mingled with the nightly breeze, gave him a chill. He shivered.

"Getting cool these evenings," he said walking to the group of volunteer deputies near the barricaded house.

Edna was about to cross Second Street when she was accosted by the black monster.

"Boy, It's a hot one!"

Edna did not answer. She stared at the traffic light above her.

"Hey Edna, you should have been at the swim party tonight. Boy, what a time!"

Edna smiled at Larry McBridy, mostly hidden inside the large black steel hearse. Red changed to green and Edna stood waiting. The black hearse pulled slowly alongside the curb. The voice came soft and pleading from the black interior.

"What'a you doing tonight?"

"Nothing. Going home." Edna wondered about the black hearse. It excited her. "What are you doing in your father's hearse?"

"Nothing, just riding 'round. All the cars are clean and dad said I could use this one. 'Course I got to be careful."

"You look funny."

"Me? Look funny?"

"You're too little for that big hearse."

"Want to take a ride?" Larry McBridy had thrown the gear into neutral.

"Where to?"

"No place. Everywhere! I'm just ridin' 'round, not doing nothing."

Edna opened the door and climbed onto the seat. Edna was in Clay Town High; Larry in St. Mary's, but they both had to face their senior year this fall. She was forbidden to ride with boys, but Edna, fascinated with the hearse and the night, overcame the fear evoked by her grandmother.

"I've never rode in a hearse before. Do you drive in funerals?"

"Sure," Larry spoke with pride. "Dad lets me drive sometimes, but I have to be careful. These aren't like ordinary cars. They're hard to steer and stop."

The hearse lurched through the yellow traffic light and Edna became fearful.

"Larry! Be careful!"

"It'll do a hundred and five. I tried it once."

"It had better not go that fast with me in it or I'll jump out."

"You mean that, don't you? You'd really jump out?" Edna was silent.

"You're a strange girl."

"I'm not strange."

"You never date."

"Maybe I don't want to."

"Maybe it's because your grandmother don't want you to."

Edna was silent again.

"I'm sorry." Larry spoke, slowing for the last traffic light before leaving town. "I don't mean half what I say."

"Grandma would have a fit if she knew I was out riding."

"And your mother? What would your mother say?"

"Oh, she does everything Grandma tells her."

"Gee, I feel sorry for you."

"Well please don't."

"But I do. You can't never have fun like us. I passed the city hall a dozen times tonight and saw you playing checkers with Gumpy."

"I like playing checkers with my uncle. He's funny and kind."

Larry wanted to confess, so he did. "I've passed that office a lot of Friday nights and I always stopped to watch you through the window, 'course I could only see your head, but gee, it was nice seeing you smile. You never smile in school."

"It's because I don't like school." Edna felt pleased that Larry

McBridy had stopped to see her through a window, but she was embarrassed. She wanted to change the subject.

"Do you like school, Larry?"

"Sure, I like it."

"But you never make the best grades. I make good grades and I don't like it."

"It's because I like school for other things besides grades. You'd like it too if your grandmother would let you go out."

"I'm out now."

"Yeah, but she don't know."

"What are you going to do after school's out?"

"Leave here."

Edna was surprised that Larry, with such a dignified identity as a mortician's son, would want to leave. She had never told anyone her secret aspiration to leave Clay Town, but now she wanted Larry to know, maybe because he had stopped to see her through a window, maybe because she felt small and unimportant inside the hearse and found that nothing really mattered from birth to death except... She slid closer to the driver. Edna hardly dared speak above a whisper.

"I'm going to leave too."

"Where you going?"

The simple acceptance by Larry excited Edna. She trusted him. But she became silent for a moment. The dream had been with her too long to have a beginning in speech.

The countryside passed unseen but felt by Edna. The highway opened before them. It was a hole in the inky black universe. Everything smelled wet as the hearse sped alongside the corn fields yawning toward the fleeting lights, then, as they passed, sinking again into the curtain of solitude. "Where to?" Larry repeated.

"I want to go to the city," Edna stared through the window. "Maybe New York."

Larry laughed. "What'd you do there?"

His arrogance made her empty herself of the hidden dreams. "I want to be a secretary, or a bartender. I don't care as long as I can live!"

Larry had difficulty holding the hearse on the open road. He had desired Edna, thinking quiet girls were more easily excited, and now his suspicions were confirmed. Now his thoughts escaped to the next turn off. It led onto an unused road and toward his favorite parking place. He became flushed, but it was not the heat of summer night which warmed Larry...

"The truth of it all is, they got it pretty well barricaded." Gumpy had not spoken until satisfying himself, walking carefully around the house"

"We'll have to rush."

The men shuffled their feet in the gravel and moved slowly back toward the police car. Harry O'Brien spoke for the men, the volunteer deputy becoming the leader.

"Can't you fire a tear gas bomb in there?"

"Now Harry, you walked around it with me. They got all the windows boarded. Where we gonna get a bomb in? Besides, there's not time."

"Well, it's pretty risky rushing in like that."

"We got to do it before long or Shaparo's gonna shoot up the street. You heard him."

"How 'bout burning it down?"

"Now come on Harry, you got better sense than that. They probably have 'nuff amo in there to blow this here block up. Don't know how they got it; it's passed me, but truth is, they got it, an' all we can do is rush 'em an' hope for the best."

"The men don't take too kindly toward that move." Harry poised his rifle against the ground as he shook his head. "It's not that they're 'fraid, but Christ, Gumpy, they ain't in the mood for gettin' shot no more'n you are."

"Shaparo gave us thirty minutes to decide to let 'em get out of town before they blow it up."

"They won't will they?"

"Now Harry, I would 'ave told you no a few minutes ago, but hell, I thought Shaparo was sane then. Now that he's shootin', it means he's gonna get out or get killed in the break."

"I think the men should pull back and let 'em get away."

Gumpy looked at Harry and smiled. Gumpy wanted to do just that. Now his cowardly thoughts were justified. Now he had the right to run. Everyone would say that he had protected the men with him. Gumpy looked down at the missing button and fingered it. He had not been asked to face barricaded criminals during the ten years with the police department of Clay Town — picking up drunks, stopping fights, investigating petty robberies — his term had passed lacking danger of sudden death, but there was danger in these chores, and there was the expectancy that death would come. "You're right, Harry. Tell 'em to go back to city hall and wait. I'll take care of things here."

"You gonna give Shaparo your car?"

"Just tell 'em to git. Hear?"

"Sure."

Harry joined the group of rifle bearing deputies.

They quickly walked away. Gumpy heard the men leave by the noise of grinding pebbles. Then Gumpy turned toward the house.

"Hey Shaparo, you know you can't get away. They'll find you out in the next county." There was no answer.

"Why don't you boys give it up now? Okay?" Moments passed.

"You can have my car." Gumpy started the police cruiser's engine and drove close to the house, climbed out, and held the keys high.

"See, I'm tossing 'em on the front seat. The others left."

"Git!"

"Sure." Gumpy threw the keys onto the seat and walked into the darkness.

Am I being a coward? No, I've done my duty all these years. No siree, I gave 'em a lot of work. He stopped in the darkness and felt the missing button again. Hell, who'm I kiddin'. They broke the law here and here's where they got to be picked up, by me. Can't run away from that no matter how I talk 'round it. Gumpy smiled through fear.

The black hearse pulled into the remote Catholic cemetery and circled around toward the rear. It was not lighted and the darkness dimmed the large statue of the crucifixion. "We're alike, Edna. I tell you we're alike. We both want to live wild."

Edna was too excited to realize the large hearse had stopped and that Larry McBridy held her tightly with his searching hands.

"Alike? Are we really alike?" Edna was confused.

"Sure we are. I want excitement and so do you. Big city, lights, all that stuff. We weren't made for Clay Town, Edna. I love you." Larry lied and he took advantage of it by kissing Edna on the lips and pulling her onto his lap. His lie led to others.

"We can go away together, be married and live together in New York, huh?"

"I love you, Larry. Please take me away!" His lie affected Edna.

She had stuffed the detective magazine beneath her and now it fell to the floor unnoticed.

"Sure. We'll go away and never come back. Just you and me and our own apartment and we'll have love every night of the week."

He kissed her again and her black skirt was above her round youthful thighs. She wanted him to love her now and let him take her away later. Larry wanted only to fuck her now. He had watched her walk in school; he had watched her grow into soft, round skin, and now he claimed her. Edna fought, not against love, but for it.

He felt it go in and the hole was hot. Gumpy reached down, but instead, he felt the missing button. He feared the hot hole. There was blood too. He felt it drying in the breeze and he became sick, vomiting fear over the gravel tar of the alley.

Shaparo's body was sprawled across the steps, lighted by gun flashes of hot yellow from near the car. The flashes made noises and Gumpy felt other hot holes in his body. He did not stop firing his revolver. The black tar came up to meet him, and there was only the heat of the holes keeping him awake. The heat passed to numbness and Gumpy fell into the depth of the blackness.

The hearse lurched through the night and Larry, his arm around Edna's shoulder, was thinking of a way to ask for the return of his class ring. Edna sat, dazed and wonderfully happy, playing with the love reward. Larry knew he must ask before she left the hearse, but he wanted to be gentle. He felt sorry for the lonely girl, but what would his friends think? What would his father say? He would leave for college next year and he knew that Edna wouldn't understand...

The Mayor

His parents migrated from Germany, but Karl Schmidt, as a child and later growing into sprawling legs, was an American. Karl had ambition as a child to become president of the United States, and while he prayed inside the arched Catholic church, Karl dreamed of commanding legions. Later, when the Clay Town High School football players battled on the field, Karl sat on the bench and dreamed of becoming a college quarterback. He tried to read but reading was not dreaming. There was action in reading and Karl feared action. There were few things which Karl could do, but he could dream, and the future before him was always pleasant in his dreams.

Karl was not a scholar. Latin and algebra came hard to him. Karl blamed his environment. His family, poor whites of the South Side, had settled in the poorer section of Clay Town. His mother kept the Schmidt home spotless and organized, but this cleanliness on the part of his mother only angered and confused Karl, for here was harmony in the middle of chaos. Mr. and Mrs. Schmidt spoke little English, and again, Karl blamed his failings on their ignorance. After graduating from Clay Town High, he became an insurance salesman, earning an independent income. Karl moved from the neat, comfortable dwelling across the tracks into a one room flat and forgot how to speak German, forgot that he came from the South Side.

It was early June when he made the speech proposing reform

in Clay Town politics. His dreams held the people. He had conversed with them, realizing the situation in Clay Town called for reform — the office holders recognized only the owners of Clay plants, ignoring workers, workers earning small incomes. Karl exaggerated the crimes, small, insignificant to officials, but the workers listened to Karl, bending forward while Karl shouted from the steps of city hall, straining ears to hear the small, black-haired German, congesting traffic along Grant Street to listen. They finally broke into riots. The ten to 15 rioters were quickly bored. Their damage amounted to a broken window in city hall. Karl talked to them and they listened. The workers could not wait until election to execute Karl's dreams for them. The acting mayor, Jim Duffy, resigned the following week, and Karl, led by a group of clay workers, entered his small yellow office, took the chair, and smiled.

Karl was bloated by the first sweets of success; born one generation out of Germany, Karl was an American. They came to his office the next day. The lawyers, the men carrying note books, men wearing black suits. They came to dictate his duties. Karl, at first, slammed his fist against the desk, then became docile and listened. Karl began to bite his fingernails while listening, and outside the workers drove home hoping their dreams would come true through the tiny German.

Karl made no more speeches to the workers. He settled back in his swivel chair and took two naps before dinner, ate in the Westway roadhouse, a restaurant and bar across from the railroad shops. There he promised individual workers that the new bill was coming and that he, Karl Schmidt, would take action at that time. At night Karl stayed away from the Westway. Too many questions were asked. Instead, he found comfort in visiting the Golding residence. Mr. Golding, owner of Clay Plant Four, had talked to him that first day, and it was Mr. Golding who had silenced Karl's commanding voice. Each night Alice Golding, the daughter, listened to Karl's dreams. She laughed, but Karl loved her laughter and he bowed his head smiling until the laughter stopped, then he went on, knowing that he made Alice Golding laugh, and laughter had become happiness for Karl. He asked her to marry him, once, twice; it became a nightly parting. His pleading brought laughter from the Clay Plant owner's daughter.

Alice began to feel the first blossoms of sweet desire and soon it fermented inside her, flowing out, permeating her nerves, and while she laughed, she desired to lay exhausted, to Karl perhaps, to any one. She walked the streets by day realizing there was no one except Karl. She submitted to his advances and allowed him to enter her. After, on the couch late at night, she laughed until Karl could hardly stand it. He begged that she marry him, and Alice laughed all the harder. He wanted her to become motherly. Alice took every precaution, telling Karl that it would be a sin to bring children by him into the world. Karl understood that an unwed mother was her fear. He submitted to her nightly orders, careful to please her every wish.

Karl Schmidt feared and loved Alice Golding. He knew that she was killing him as her father had destroyed his strength that first day of victorious defeat. Alice Golding was his future, his dream. Her father was power. Karl no longer desired to lead but stand behind the iron fists of power. Therefore he submitted to her nightly orders. He sought out her face by day, but Alice would not recognize him on the street. He knew it was because she didn't want people to say that the mayor was friendly with the Goldings. She had baited him with another lie.

Karl was not without fear. The workers began to stare at him, then speak harsh words about Karl, then bumped against him on the street. Karl gathered his friends, men of drink, men without fear, men without work. He appointed them auxiliary policemen. Some workers called Karl's friends shock-troops; others called them legionnaires, but the auxiliary police surrounded the tiny mayor and made him happy. They opened doors, took his coat, cleaned his desk, smiled when he was happy, frowned at the slightest mishap, and never laughed openly. Laughter was reserved for Alice Golding. Karl once tried to bring a bodyguard to the Golding home, or rather, an auxiliary policeman, a burly farmer who had recently lost his farm. The man's name was Tom Shanks. Alice quickly sent the man away. She laughed at Karl for inviting him.

"You frightened little man," she laughed. "Must you bring your boobs to watch you make love?"

That night Alice regretted sending the handsome, homely farmer away.   Her love was outgrowing the tiny mayor. Each Friday night Karl drove her, in the Golding Oldsmobile, to the drive-in movie, five miles outside Clay Town, and each Friday, Karl asked Alice if his auxiliary police could follow.

"Why, my silly?" But Alice was happy that the men would be near. Later she wanted to meet them, stare into their eyes, and explore their thoughts.

"The bill comes up to town council next week." Karl stopped.

"And?"

"The bill I fought against. It got me into office, Alice. I said I'd oppose it, stop it, and they believed me. I said I'd get more industry for Clay Town, in fact, I promised that I had talked to others, outside, who wanted to start industry here. In that way it would raise wages and give the men fair working agreements instead of giving all the power to the clay factories."

"Do you want to stop tradition, my silly little mayor?" Alice did not laugh.

"No. I'm for the bill now. It's that some workers think that a city requirement keeping all industry out so the clay plants can control prices, control wages, control everything — they think it wrong, my sweet."

"But do you think it wrong, Karl? Do you oppose tradition and all that has made this town?"

"The town is failing, my sweet. No one wants clay pipes anymore. Construction companies are using cement pipes. The factories aren't working full capacity."

"Then I assume you are against the bill?"

Karl thought about her father then about the Golding home, then about Alice and the couch.

"No, I'm very much for it, and it cannot pass without my approval. That's why my auxiliary police must stay near me, until then at least."

"Do you want them to watch us making love?"

"No, of course not."

"Do you have control over them? The big one, I mean?" Alice smiled.

"Of course I do."

"Then I don't mind if he watches."

"But, my sweet, it's not decent. "

Tom Shanks watched because Alice wanted him to watch, and Karl felt more embarrassed, more dominated, but the tiny black-haired German respected Alice's wishes. He submitted to her will, knowing it was the way of the Goldings. Tom Shanks watched and desired. He wanted to use his hands, his body. Alice became the earth and he wanted to plow. The hard muscles of the farm man wanted, desired. He had difficulty obeying the tiny mayor, but Tom looked long and steady into the eyes of Alice, desiring, wanting to know the secret he inwardly knew and could not know or explain to himself. Being recently from the work of the earth, Tom did not know the ways of the town so he rested his hand around hers and told Alice he wanted to know and be known. Alice laughed and Tom was happy.

Karl began to fear Tom Shanks. Fear soon became hate. He wanted to dismiss Tom from the auxiliary police, but Alice laughed. Soon the hate was returned and Tom became rude to the mayor in Alice's presence. Of course, Tom was, at last, forbidden to watch Alice's ritual, although she complained to Karl that he, the mayor, had no control over his own men. She laughed and allowed Karl to have his way for once.

It was Friday as Karl drove the Golding Oldsmobile toward town. Alice's hand rested on his lap.

"Must we travel the old road?"

"Where's your German blood, Karl?" Alice laughed. "Such a silly, silly man to lead a town."

"Okay, we'll go the back way then."

"That's more becoming a mayor."

"But Alice, this morning I told them."

"Yes, daddy told me." Alice, puffing a cigarette, watched blackness pass. "They didn't like you approving the bill, did they?"

"Can we take the main road?"

"No."

The car sped past the slumbering fires of plant #6 and still Karl was frightened. Then there was no road left. Karl hesitantly applied the brakes and the large car rolled to a stop.

"They'll get me, Alice. They'll get me now," Karl stared at the tree blocking the road. Its branches sprawled across the gray pavement.

"It's because of you that they've got me," Karl sat and tried to think.

"But where are my auxiliary police? They should be following."

Alice turned and saw that no car followed. She laughed. "You'll have to crawl tonight, won't you Karl? I gave them the night off. Do you know what those workers can do to a silly little man?"

Alice felt hatred toward her lover. She realized she had always hated him for his weakness. She submitted out of self punishment to one weaker than herself. Now she knew. She hated him, but she hated herself more. Now she knew. She was free of self-hatred. She had paid her penance, and she wondered what would happen next. She was free to act. First she must make him the ugly little man that he was.

"They'll castrate you. They'll hang you from the highest tree."

Karl continued to tremble and Alice laughed, not from hate, but from pity.

"You shouldn't have promised them things you couldn't give. Now should you have, Mr. Mayor?"

"It was your fault! You made me! I wanted to help them. I promised to help them, but you, and your father, and the others. You forced me!"

"We did not force you, Karl. You came to us because you are a silly, weak little man who needs help. You have to take our gifts to help yourself. You made one speech which was not you and they thought you their savior. Yes, I see you now as the silly, little, funny man that you are. You should have stayed in that hovel on the South Side."

Karl wanted to cry, but even more, he wanted to strike out against the power beside him. He wanted to call Alice a dirty name, the worst name, something that would hurt her. "You are the lowest whore in this town, my sweet." It was not the word whore that angered Alice in so much as Karl's tone of voice. The word should have been uttered in anger, but Karl said it gently as if soothing her, and it became ugly.

"And you are a German whore-monger who thinks of himself as a man and a leader!" Alice laughed in defense.

"Worse than that, my sweet, I'm a pimp to the rich and powerful. I'm your pimp. I pimp for the lowest whore of all."

"I hope they cut your balls off!"

Alice pointed toward the approaching men. There was no escape for Karl. He might have backed the car up and tried to return to the main road, but it was useless. They would eventually find him out in the dark.

"I'll show you who's a leader!" Karl got out of the car and stood straight. The blood came to his head, blood of centuries, and for a moment he was not Karl Schmidt of America.

"You there!" he barked. "What is the meaning of this?"

"You know, Mister Mayor! You tricked us!" The men started walking slowly, hesitantly toward Karl. He waited until they were within a few feet from him then lifted his hand. They stopped automatically at the silent order.

"You're fools! We are fools together. We have been tricked, and you must know why!" There was silence, and Karl felt that this was not time for silence.

"Well? Do you know who has tricked us? It isn't me. If I tricked you, I must surely know that I would pay at your anger, so it can't be me who would trick you. Then who has tricked us? Answer me!" The seven men muttered and Karl sought out the eyes of Tom Shanks.

"Shanks! You have seen her treachery!" Then he turned to the others.

"Here, in this car, laughing at all of us is our downfall. I tell you it is true because it is true. She has tricked you and she has tricked me. I wanted to kill the bill! I was elected by you to resist the bill, but she tricked me into believing I must rest on her arm and beg her security. Do you know what I'm going to do now that I know? Well? Do you?"

"You're gonna damn well pay for it!" Tom Shanks said cruelly.

"Ah yes. I must pay tonight for my error. But tomorrow I will personally kill the bill. I will bring industry and jobs for you into

Clay Town. I will break their control, and her spell over me will be broken."

"Are we gonna listen to this shit?" Shanks advanced then stopped. No one followed. It wasn't Karl's words which stopped the men. It was his attitude, sure of himself, standing straight, Karl looked at the workers and they fell back to the fallen tree.

"You gonna follow me?" Tom Shanks turned on them.

"Yes, listen to him. He is under her spell." Karl continued. "She has duped him and you'll follow willingly, molesting innocent people, even a mayor, your mayor and molesting him. This means prison, but you'll follow because you no longer believe in me."

Alice was out of the car and standing beside Tom Shanks .

"Kill him! He has betrayed you!" she shouted to the others. But Karl continued and his controlled voice left hers in the night.

"I must make you believe in me again. I've told you who's tricked me. Now I'll show you where my faith lies." Karl, with straight, confident steps, approached Alice and Tom. He slapped her across the cheek, not with might but enough force to be heard by the others. They moved but did not rush forward. Amazed and bewildered, they looked on.

"And you, Shanks, are under her spell. It must be broken."

Reaching up, Karl slapped Tom hard across the face and the farmer, instead of grabbing up the tiny mayor, stepped back.

"Get him, Tom! He's afraid!" Alice shouted.

Karl, to stop her voice, slapped her again, harder, sending her to the ground. Shanks retreated to the others.

"Go home!" Karl shouted. "Here is trouble. You're good men, not robbers and criminals. Go home!"

Karl turned his back on the men like a matador sure of his bull. He did not know if it was the bewilderment of the men or the approaching lights of another car that sent the men scurrying away. Minutes later, Karl stood supreme above Alice. She cried, still lying on the dirty pavement.

"Get up whore!" Alice pulled herself up without Karl's help. "Get into the car." Alice obeyed.

"Having trouble?" the voice came from the car which had approached behind the Golding Oldsmobile. Karl walked toward the fallen tree.

"No, nothing I can't handle." Karl pushed the tree from the road and returned to the Golding car. "It's passable now. Don't know how that tree got there. It was probably kids."

The big steel moved forward and Karl had control over it. Alice sat small opposite Karl. He began to laugh at Alice in a new, cruel tone. "You small, insignificant bitch. Why do you meddle in things you know nothing about?"

He reached across the emptiness of seat and grabbed her ear, pulling Alice close to him. His fingers hurt her, but after he released the pinching grip, her ear lobe felt hot and pleasant and she felt the pleasure all the way to town.

"We will be married this fall, won't we, Alice?" She did not answer but nodded her head. "We'll be married and raise Golding children with Schmidt blood."

He drove to his shabby apartment. For the first time in the strange courtship, with the rise of Karl Schmidt and Alice Golding, the woman beside him submitted silently, willingly.

Farewell St. Mary's

The entire block along First Street, between Sherman and Cross, was owned by the Catholic Church and dominated by Father Ralph Cromley who inhabited a mammoth body and fiery temper. An old three story rambling school building squatted at one end, with a one story four room high school across the asphalt school ground. A large red-brick church comprised the other end with a basement beneath for meetings and events, between, squatted the rectory, next the church then the convent next to the school, shaded by a large elm tree from the courtyard.

Gary Delaney walked along First Street on his way to a feared but necessary meeting with Father Cromley in the pastor's rectory. He stumbled on one of the many cracks along the street, caught his balance, and cursed for taking that last drink of vodka before leaving the house.

"Good evening, coach," the housekeeper, Jo Ann Dudley spoke opening the door.

Father Cromley shouted from inside. "If that's the new coach, bring him in. Immediately."

"He's in the study," she answered as the booming voice of Father Cromley overwhelmed hers.

"Did I do something wrong? I just arrived today," Gary said with his eyes shut against the raging rampant of vocal river flowing on white river strength.

"It's just that nobody does anything right," Jo Ann answered trying to calm the nervous coach. "Father is not in a good mood this evening."

"Neither am I. We haven't unpacked yet." Gary gritted his teeth following Jo Ann into the old but clean study.

"Come in! Come in!" Father Cromley shouted above his reading glasses, leaning over a model of a cardboard school building resting on the table. Then he waved Jo Ann away. "Those who stand on ceremony around here do not survive."

"You wanted to see me?" Gary stretched his hand toward the hefty priest who ignored the invitation.

"This model represents our new school. It's half paid for, half in my dreams. Five years it's taken to get this far. The parish is rotten poor," he peaked over his glasses. "Do you understand?"

"You want a new school and need money to build it."

Father Cromley gave one of his seldom nods. "You're at least savvy. That's why I hired you even if you have bottle problems." Gary's face remained hardened. It was now or never to stand up to this pompous dynamo.

"Look, Father. I don't need to be hassled. We haven't unpacked yet, and I'm not an alcoholic!"

Father Cromley turned and towered over Gary. "Your drinking problems don't worry me. That's why I got you cheap. What does concern me is that you start practice tomorrow at 10 a.m. sober. And stay that way!"

"What does that have to do with your school?"

Father Cromley turned his attention back to the model on the table as if dismissing this alcoholic from his inner circle of thoughts.

"Fifteen kids will show up for that practice. That's not enough for two teams. We don't own enough equipment for all of them as it is, but never mind that. You're going to take those kids and turn in a winning season. That's the shot in the arm this school needs. They love football here, and the winner collects all, the loser, not enough money for a chalk board."

"Father? Aren't you a bit presumptuous?" Gary walked around pretending to admire the cardboard edifice.

"I know exactly what I'm talking about," Father Cromley answered as he leaned down to adjust a cardboard tree in the make-pretend school yard. "I've brought those kids along for the past five years, since the eighth grade. They're sons of coal miners, sewer pipe workers and railroad section hands. They're good kids, but animals on the field."

"Animals don't win games," Gary replied.

Father Cromley moved close to Gary's face and held up a fist. "Delaney! See this ring! My brother gave it to me. It's a monsignor's ring. I want that title."

"And to do that you need a school named after you."

Father Cromley turned away and looked out the window. "No. Not named after me. Built by me. If we haven't started construction this year they will consolidate the high school, and it will be moved to another town, leaving us with a grade school."

"Why are you telling me this?" Gary started taking account of the cardboard in front of him.

Father Cromley was back in his face. "I believe in putting everything up front, and I trust your discretion, especially when you need a winning season as much, if not more, than I do. This talk is between the two of us, no one else, not even Father Reed, your new assistant. Remember. I can fire you dead on the spot. It's in the contract."

"Thanks for the pep talk."

Again Father Cromley's eyes looked up over his glasses. "It's not a pep talk. It's a warning!"

Practice was held at one end of Blacksmith Pond, a low scruffy land several blocks down a cinder road from the school on First Street. The sprawling bottoms was skirted by a muddy brown creek, which often overflowed. No one had laid claim to this fallow field so Father Cromley used it for the past four years. In the distance the players could see the stadium belonging to the Clay Town public school. It was rented for their home games, but they spent most game nights on the road playing bigger and better equipped teams around the state.

Waiting for the new coach to appear, some of the fifteen players were taking laps as fullback, Corny MacNeff and end, Grover McFadden, reclined on the soft earth of the sidelines.

"Shit, I don't want to be out here!" Corny stuck a stripped blade of grass in his mouth. "Summer's not even over."

"Father Cromley would bump your head in if you didn't show," Grover answered.

"Father Cromley sucks ice cubes!"

"He might be a bad ass, but he coached a tough season last year."

"We dropped two," Corny rolled over onto his back and gazed at the last dazzlement of summer's sun.

"Yeah. Class A schools," Grover rolled over on his side. "They had more guys on the team than we have in our town."

The conversation was interrupted by Titter Bee, a tough, bow-legged guard and coal-miner's son.

"You two still on vacation?" He spit chewing tobacco at Corny's feet.

"Jesus Christ, Titter!" Corny jumped to his feet. "You got a filthy mouth! We ain't down in no clay mine."

"Don't fun with me, Corny. I get good money for that work. Better'n the sewer pipe sweat houses! Want a chew?" He offered them a bag produced from his sock.

"Shit no. I don't want my teeth to fall out."

"You guys should chew. Spit at 'em in the game. Smarts the eyes. Pow," Titter Bee flexed an elbow at them.

"Yea. What about the game when you swallowed it?" Grover sat up laughing and imitating sickness by doubling up. "Hey Father! I'm sick! I'm real sick!"

"Wasn't funnin'. I was sick. Here comes Father Pussy Cat. Let's get our laps in." Titter Bee ran away a little too fast, Grover thought.

"The new coach didn't say nothing 'bout laps. Right Grover?"

"Father Cromley did. He'll be down to kick ass, you can count on that," Grover rose as Father Reed, a slim young man wearing his priestly frock, walked toward them.

"I'm not budgin' till the new coach is here," Corny replied with indignation.

"Good morning, Grover, Cornelius. Are you ready for the new season?"

"What's the new coach like, Father?" Corny asked.

Father Reed watched as several players finished their laps. "Are you finished with your laps?"

"Haven't started," Corny answered as he sat down. "We're waiting for the coach."

"I am the assistant," Father Reed folded his arms.

"You want we should do laps?" Grover asked with the sound of innocence.

"Something like that."

Gary Delany, wearing a gray jump suit and football shoes jogged past Father Reed and kicked Corny, who jumped up ready to fight, but the coach stood him down.

"Don't ever lie down on a practice field!" he shouted.

"You got no right kicking me!"

"Get your ass out on that field and do ten fast laps," Gary said, then turned to Grover. "You too!"

"Welcome to St. Mary's, Coach." Grover said before joining Corny on the run.

"Fast ones," Gary shouted then turned to Father Reed who was wide-eyed and slack-jawed.

"The whole team saw that."

"Good, then they won't fall asleep."

"I'm Father Reed, your assistant." Father Reed said holding out his hand.

Gary shook the extended hand firmly. "Father Cromley mentioned that you have never played football."

"I consider it to be a brutal sport unworthy of a civilized nation."

"Why did you volunteer to be an assistant?"

"Father Cromley strongly suggested it."

"Father Cromley runs St. Mary's like a feudal state," Gary turned and walked toward the gathered team as Father Reed followed.

"You should not have kicked Cornelius. He's very sensitive."

"What are the others like?"

"Brutish, crude, ignorant, and sensitive."

"We'll have to do something about the sensitivity. Is there any loyalty, team spirit?"

"They appreciate winning games, if that is what you mean. It makes them heroes to the girls."

Gary stopped and looked at the gathered players. "What about disciplinary problems?"

"Not with Father Cromley as pastor. There is one thing I wish you would mention to them. They believe cussing reflects manliness." Gary stared Father Reed in the face. "Do you want me to tell them not to cuss?" He emphasized the me and them.

"It would set an example."

"Where's the stadium?"

"You're standing on it when we can't rent the public school's facility over there."

"Anything else I should know?"

"They have a tendency to lift items. Most of that paraphernalia has been confiscated from opposing teams who have lost more than games. And they wear iron cleats on their shoes painting them black. They also chew tobacco, and I have smelled alcohol more than once."

Gary blew a whistle tied around his neck. The team trotted over.

They surrounded Gary who walked around inspecting each player as he shouted. "I'm Gary Delaney. Coach to you. There are some commandments I want to pass along. First. Every time one of you gentlemen cusses it's three laps. Second. No drinking, or doping, or late hours."

"That's three things, Coach." Corny spoke after finishing his laps and approaching the gathering.

"Third. No mouthing back. Three laps for anybody who speaks out of line to Father Reed or myself."

"How 'bout Father Cromley?" Titter asked.

"What's your name?"

"Titter Bee."

"You just bought yourself three laps when practice is over. Any other volunteers to accompany Titter? Where in the hell did you get that name?"

"My old man wanted me to be different."

"He sure is!" The quarterback, Paul Rossi, laughed.

"Fourth. No one misses practice unless you have two broken legs. Five. No one is late for practice. Six, at practice no one sits, stands or lies down. Laps for anyone who does. Seven, any gripes come directly to me. Eight, you'll do everything Father Reed and I tell you. Nine. You put everything you have into practice. Ten, we win every game we play this season. Any questions?"

"What's in it for us?" The tackle, Billy Cossetti, asked.

"Fame, fortune, women and the chance to get out of here. If what I hear is right, this school will produce one of the top football teams in the state. That means recognition. Recognition means offers from colleges. You give me wins, I'll give you all that."

"Can I ask a question?" Larry asked with his right hand in the air. Gary nodded and he lowered his hand. "Why has Father Cromley lined up some of the biggest and toughest schools in the state? Christ! We're a class C school!"

Gary walked up to Larry and spoke into his face.

"You don't get recognized playing second rate teams. And Christ is not a name you throw around. Join Titter Bee and Corny for three laps at the conclusion of practice." Gary turned to the others. Take two more laps around, fast ones, then line up for pass reception."

Father Reed walked up to Gary as the players began their laps. "Thank you for cutting short their cussing, but there is one thing which perplexes me. Your commandments didn't mention sportsmanship?"

Gary kicked at a piece of turf. "You don't talk about sportsmanship. You live it."

After practice Father Reed walked slowly and painfully to the rectory. He could feel every muscle stretched in the practice. He wished to limp straight to the small second floor bedroom, but Father Cromley would want a moment to fifteen minutes of his time. The study door was open and Father Reed walked in attempting not to hobble. Father Cromley sat at his desk staring at pledge cards.

"The practice session went well," Father Reed said softly. Father Cromley jumped to his feet and began to flail his arms. "Well my ass! I saw what was happening through the telescope."

"What went wrong?"

"Everything went wrong! It was the first day of practice. You don't engage in head-on tackling, machine blocking and scrimmage! They shouldn't have been wearing uniforms!"

Father Reed walked to the telescope, which pointed down toward the practice field. "It was hot."

Father Cromley joined him. "Those kids will never make the first game let alone win."

"That is the first time I have ever heard you refer to them as kids. What happened to animals?"

"Never mind what I call them," he said adjusting the telescope. "What did they think about the new coach?"

Father Reed heaved his shoulders in a "who knows" attitude. "He set standards, was firm yet gentle in a strange sort of way. He worked alongside them, sweated as much as they, and didn't cuss, much."

"That's what you thought about him. What did the team think?"

Father Reed cleared his throat as if to give the question plausibility. "I detected that they missed your guidance. In fact, Cornelius MacNeff asked why had you hired a coach. Over all, they respected him, but missed you. There was one problem though. Paul Rossi broke his helmet."

Father Cromley turned on his assistant coach. "Does the coach know how much helmets costs?"

"He mentioned something about buying them wholesale and complimented the two players for their effort by tackling so hard."

Father Cromley huffed away his anger. "The coach can take the cost out of his salary. I didn't hire him to spend money!"

Father Reed looked down at his shoes. "Talking about money, Father. Do you think there is enough in the athletic fund to buy me a pair of football shoes and a jump suit?"

Father Cromley returned to the cardboard model of the

school. "It needs bushes here, along the front. Those damn architects never supply landscaping. That's what makes the finished product. Perhaps Jo Ann can make some bushes. She's good at that sort of thing."

"Goodnight Father." Father Reed turned toward the door.

"Have the coach order you a pair of shoes and a jump suit since he knows how to get them wholesale."

"Thank you," Father Reed answered with a smile.

"Don't thank me. You just spent your coaching salary."

Outside the room Father Reed said in a loud voice. "Should have asked for more."

Day after day, practice after practice, Father Cromley paced between the telescope and his desk. They had won four important games. The pledge money was mounting as the pastor combed through the town ever alert to possible contributions. Something was wrong. Father Cromley had lost control. It was no longer his game. Then one Friday afternoon Father watched through the telescope as Corny tackled the second string player called Pinty and threw him to the ground. The body bounced twice from the force of the fall. He did not get up. The other players were upset with Corny. Father Cromley stormed out of his office heading toward his black New Yorker.

On the field, the coach and Father Reed ran to Pinty where Corny knelt beside the unconscious warrior. "You okay, Pinty? Pinty?"

The coach grabbed Pinty's belt and rocked him hard as the wind returned to the small guy. "Get the smelling salts, Father!" He reached down and rocked Pinty again.

"Hey coach! I'm sorry. I didn't mean to do that. I was just pissed because he was trying to fake me out."

"Don't be sorry!" The coach spoke into Corny's face. "You'll make Pinty look like an ass. This kid has more guts than the team put together, and you won't help him by being sorry. Now get back in line and keep it moving!"

Corny ran back to the now broken line of players. "Okay you knotholes! The coach is right. Pinty don't want sympathy. I was wrong, but this is football so let's play it."

"You carry the ball! Me and Ronny will do the tackling. Okay Mr. Big Guy?" The tackle, Jimmy Manno, weighed two hundred and twenty pounds without much fat. Adding Ronny, it would be a four hundred pound tackle. Corny knew he had to do it, but was saved by the presence of a ten year old black New Yorker Chrysler, which cascaded Father Cromley onto the practice field.

"The practice is over!" Father Cromley shouted.

"The hell it is!" The coach turned on the priest, who had taunted him and the team game after game running up and down the sidelines.

"The hell it isn't!"

The coach, weighing one hundred sixty pounds, approached the two hundred and thirty pound priest. "Get off my turf and stay off!"

"I happen to own this field!"

"No you don't. The catholic church owns this field!"

"I am a representative of the catholic church!"

Father Reed stepped between the two men. "Father Cromley! Please! You are out of line!"

The players cheered.

"I'm what?" The priest Cromley glared down at Father Reed, his young assistant.

"Please, Father. We can discuss this later. Do you want this team to win tomorrow night or don't you? If you do, please leave the field."

Father Cromley turned on his heels without a word spoken

and climbed into the large black car. The coach returned to help Pinty and Father Reed ran to him.

"Coach. May I have permission to start the players on their laps?"

"You do."

Father Reed blew his whistle and shouted. "Everyone! Take your laps," then looked at the coach. "You have a penance of three laps for one hell."

"So does Father Cromley." They both laughed.

Later that evening, Father Reed entered the church sanctuary and knelt next to Father Cromley. "Jo Ann said I would find you here. I'm sorry about the confrontation on the practice field."

Father Cromley did not look at the young priest. "You're shaping up. You might even survive."

"It was a delicate moment," Father Reed answered looking at the altar. "Too much was happening. There was no right way to cope with the situation."

Father Cromley glanced at his assistant. "Do you want forgiveness? Penance?"

Father Reed continued to stare at the altar. "Do you feel animosity toward me for stepping in?"

Father Cromley looked at his folded hands. "I have a mean, strong, determined temper. It's helped to refurbish this house of God. It's helped to build that team, to keep this poverty parish alive. It's helped to raise the money for a new school. I'd advise you to cultivate one."

Father Reed continued to look at the altar. "There are other ways. You have not answered my question."

Father Cromley lowered his head. "Yes I have answered your question. Now if you will let me pray in peace."

The opening kickoff against Midtown left two of their players down. The rest of the game was brutal with St. Mary's emerging unscathed with a 33 to zero win. Hoppersburg was a Class A school with tall strong farmer-types as ends and backfield. St. Mary's punched through them with a 21 to zero defeat. Valley High and Colesville, Class B teams, suffered defeats as the coach polished the skills of his team.

Father Cromley continued to attend games driving his black New Yorker behind the battered bus. Three parishioners rode along, all contributors to the school fund. Father Reed rode on the bus.

During the games, Father Cromley would follow the team up and down the sidelines, quick to correct any infraction committed on the field, quicker to shout instructions to his team, or taunt the referees. There were two confrontations with Gary during the Putsmorth game. One lasted four minutes and was only concluded because St. Mary's had made a touchdown. He continued to criticize the coach at every opportunity of an impeding disaster. But the team won despite penalty calls caused by the rantings of Father Cromley. He wanted to show the coach, the team, and the parish that he was still in charge, that this was his team, created from the anarchy of eighth grade animals.

It was the last game of the season and the team had a chance of becoming Class B, state champions. This, despite their being a Class C school. Only St. Jude remained. They were the arch rival, a larger school fifteen miles away, but playing at St. Mary's rented stadium.

The snow had stopped. In the locker room below the grade school, the team was packing their equipment for the trek to Clay Town High's stadium a few blocks away. The coach stepped out of the locker room looking for Father Reed and spied Father Cromley standing, looking down at him in the school yard. The coach started to turn, not wanting a confrontation with the priest, but Cromley called out. "Delaney! Come here!"

"I'm busy." The coach looked up toward the priest who stood at the end of an ice slide, which children had made earlier in the day.

"I said come here!" The priest pointed to the ground in front of him.

"You can't order me around!"

"The hell I can't!"

"The hell you can!"

"You come here or you're fired!"

The coach started to run toward the big priest standing determined above him. He jumped onto the ice of the slide and coasted on momentum up toward the priest. "You asked for it all season, you son-of-a-bitch!"

At the end of the slide the coach connected a fist to the mouth of Cromley. The priest went down hard against the snow.

"Damn you!" Father Cromley shouted looking toward the night sky with blood gushing from his mouth.

The coach turned and walked away toward his home, across from the church, to the comfort of his wife and child. The home was owned by the church and they lived there at the benevolence of Father Cromley. At the church he turned up the street toward the locker room. He could not go home. At the door to the locker room, he took a deep breath of cold air and entered; then stood lost in the middle of the room. He held up his bloody hand with tears in his eyes and shouted at his team. "You guys get over to the stadium on the double. You run all the way. I just hit your priest! I didn't want to, but he asked for it. All season he asked for it. You get your asses to that stadium and win! Do you hear me! You've got to win this game!"

They picked up their bundles and ran out of the locker room toward the stadium. Not one player glanced into the school yard where an ambulance was parked. They passed the police car which pulled in next to the ambulance. Bob Denton, hefty friend and successor to Gumpy, climbed out and joined Father Reed as he walked next to the stretcher. "You'd better follow them kids to the stadium. Could be trouble, Father."

"Thanks, Bob. I shouldn't have told Father Cromley about the consolidation. I should have waited. Bad timing."

"What consolidation?"

"St. Mary's will be consolidated into St. Jude's."

"They're going up there, huh? Want me to arrest the coach? Guess he went out of his mind hitting a priest."

"Let's not press charges. This is a private matter."

"You sure, Father? The coach could get in more trouble if he's stepped off the deep side."

"You can talk to him. He's probably in the locker room. Tell him when he feels like it, we're expecting him at the game." The assistant coach, now head coach, ran after his team.

Bob entered the locker room and walked over to where Gary sat on a broken chair.

"You okay, coach?"

"Have you come to arrest me?"

"Naw. Father Reed said not to press charges. Don't think Father Cromley will either when he comes 'round. He's tough but not that way."

"I didn't intend to hit him. He wouldn't stop hassling me."

"It happens sometimes. You don't feel like punching anyone else tonight, do you?"

The coach shook his head.

"Father Reed said they would be waiting for you at the game when you come 'round."

"Yeah. It's time to go."

Grover McFadden limped into the rectory courtyard early the next morning and found Father Reed leaving the rectory for church.

"Are you serving mass this morning?" Father Reed asked.

"Filling in for Corny. He's too sore to be going anywhere. Sorry we lost, Father. How's Father Cromley?"

"They brought him home from the hospital last night. He was resting comfortably. We can't find the coach. I've looked everywhere."

Grover opened the door of the sanctuary. "I heard he left town. Just like that. Left. We heard about the consolidation. Guess we're the last class of St. Mary's."

"There will be a grade school," Father Reed answered as he entered the church.

Grover shook his head. "Not the same. Not the same."

Part II
AUTUMN

The Parker

Jimmy Wilson was not like other Clay Town teenagers. As a child he had neither collected baseball pictures, match covers, or bottle caps. Later, much later, in his teens, when other boys were secretly collecting pin-up pictures and pornographic magazines, which they wisely hid from parents, Jimmy collected only thoughts and dreams. These weird collections became manifest and crept into the light of reality in his occasional journey to the deserted lovers lane of Sewer Pipe Factory #5, where other teenagers lost themselves in aggressive actions of dark, nightly love. Jimmy, however, could not fondle and charm his partners. He sat and became aware of night surrounding him, sometimes forgetting that life breathed beside him.

When reminded about social obligations, namely attention due the female across the seat, Jimmy became overwhelmed with shame. Why can't I love like others? He pondered this question concerning aggressive love while staring into the woods behind Plant #5. The answer was as evasive as the hidden and primordial existence of those woods.

"Why can't you love like other guys?" A breathless Miss Rosaland Hecker, excited by a harvest moon, asked one night, "Jimmy, are you a queer?"

The mention of perversion bothered Jimmy. He had never considered its consequences before. It was a dirty word his companions yelled at foreigners from the city and half-wits like Dag.

Now it had been applied to him — the mark of shame. Jimmy did not blame Rosaland. She didn't know, but neither did Jimmy understand his vigilances behind Plant #5. He was a poet, but Jimmy did not understand nor write poetry. And so the trips with female defenders narrowed to a small, tight-skinned girl a year behind him in Clay Town High. Dorothy Collins was not without beauty and charm — she had almost become cheerleader the year before as a freshman. Her long black hair was a delight to the male students. In grade school, growing pains made them tug it. Later in high school, it became a sea which begged a swim by hands, but Dorothy had received the reputation of "a queer girl" from her own sex. She ignored those around her, dreaming dreams beyond. It was quite natural that she would eventually date Jimmy, and the first date led to others. Dorothy enjoyed the trips to Plant #5 as she struggled to bring Jimmy's thoughts back inside the car. Soon he was telling them to her. First with reluctance, then gradually his voice took hold and began to drown Dorothy in those deep, deep thoughts which teen-agers are not expected to possess in a small town.

"Sitting here watching them trees does things to me," Jimmy glanced nervously at Dorothy, who only stared into the night.

"It's not like the other guys. They're after one thing. You know that, don't you?" He didn't stop. He couldn't stop.

"But it's like watching a whole world pass before me. I mean it. Sure, there's nothing out there, but I can hear and see a whole world passing. Autumn tides that change man's electrons and the burning electricity behind nature."

Soon Dorothy was dreaming and watching that world. Sometimes Jimmy interrupted himself, introducing strange people into the darkness outside, characters and worlds they had seen at the Clay Town movie house. The actors seemed to trip across darkness somewhere before them or somewhere within them. It was natural that Jimmy's and Dorothy's world would expand outside Clay Town.

"I'm going to up and leave someday. You watch! I'm going to get out of here. I got to get out of here! This town's dead! It's dying for me."

"Once there was a town, now there's only machines and empty skin. Out here, in these woods, is where I live, out here on Friday nights, with you. It's not real back in town. The other guys got football and basketball and baseball and talking to girls at Eisels, but me, I got to work in Dad's store. I don't want to sell cosmetics and medicine. I, I, want to see things happen!"

Jimmy and Dorothy saw another world on Friday nights — a sustaining world of darkness and light without middle dullness to fade and dull their imaginations — a scene of youth and dreams. Dorothy began to share Jimmy's interest in travel and adventure books.

"Wiley Post, that's the kind of guy I want to be. Just to fly off into them mountains of Alaska and never return. I wish they wouldn't have found his and Will Rogers' bodies, then I could think he had only crashed and lived up there in the mountains."

More than once, Jimmy turned to Dorothy and asked, "Am I...queer for thinking that?"

Her smile assured him that she did not think so, and Jimmy immediately dived on into other adventures; men and names passed through the woods.

"Really, Glen Miller was a basket case. Sure, he didn't get killed in the channel during the war. He's still alive but they keep it a secret."

"'On The Waterfront' could have taken place on the streets of Clay Town. Our football team is tough, and the clay workers are just as rough if not rougher than those longshoremen, and I raised pigeons in my back yard."

Jimmy talked on and Dorothy listened, believing.

Their hands met one autumn night and each following Friday night as Jimmy drove to the secluded lane. Their hands groped across the seat to touch, then grasp.

Soon Jimmy's hand was touching Dorothy's skirt. It rested on her lap with her hand in his, pressing gently, unaware, against her hot skin beneath the cloth. Later, his hand found her bare skin. Her hand was no longer necessary to comfort him. He had found her flesh. The hand could not be still. It began to express what once his thoughts had expressed. On Friday nights the hand began to smooth the hot flesh, gripping her thigh, pinching gently, running his fingers around the elastic panties. On Friday nights it fondled the nylons, dug at the tight girdle, and Jimmy began to speak less. He did not want this. Dorothy did not want this. But the movements of the hand seemed to be controlled by something beyond the woods.

That fall the hand found hers out in the halls of school. Students watched, wondered, and talked. "The queer ones got something on."

Jimmy heard their whispers and denied their remarks with vigorous head shaking.

"'Tain't so. We just talk. That's all. Talk."

He resented the students' remarks. Their sexual implications was the work of the hand he no longer controlled.

"You gettin' any? Hey Jim, gettin' any?" He blushed and that night he talked to his father.

"I got to get away. I want to go away and study."

His father laughed and called in Mrs. Wilson, who did not laugh as much. Jimmy listened abstractedly to his father's remarks, remarks similar to those of the students — telling him that he must accept it. That Dorothy was part of it.

"Of course you got to discipline yourself, Jim. There's a lot of trouble if you let your desires run away with you. Now take that Saxton couple last year. He didn't even finish school, and..."

Jimmy drove Dorothy to the woods that night. They both recognized at once that the world of the woods was dead. Had they killed it, or had it been the hand?

They sat silently in the car and soon her legs were pressing the hand tighter and tighter between flesh. The snow fell against steel and the hand worked until the sweat steamed the windows and froze the woods from view. Physically they were no longer seated apart. Dorothy bruised her head against the door handle. Jimmy bumped his head against the steering wheel and his backside felt the bite of cold air. She bent to his kisses, submitting to each added wave of flesh against flesh and Jimmy felt her helplessly beneath him giving way into a crumpled heap. It maddened him to find her there. He became cruel, beating against her, harder, harder, until the steel rocked and she screamed with pleasure and could not stop. At last she collapsed into the heap beneath him and felt the cold plastic seat cover against his wet sweating face. His breath was thick and he felt the frost settle. Dorothy sobbed. He had expected as much. He began and wailed in a new masculine voice which was not familiar to Jimmy. He wanted to scream, "I love you," but words would not come. They had passed with the woods. Now he felt shame where once he had felt joy.

After the sex act, Dorothy sat upright. She stared again before her, but this time the steamed windows offered only a blank white frost. She wiped the glass but the frost returned quickly covering the small hole of abstraction.

"Let's talk." She knew that something had gone. Now she wanted to regain it.

"Sure, let's talk," Jimmy muttered. He chuckled and marked the window with his index finger. "See, you can make figures in the frost." His finger unconsciously made a circle. Dorothy did not notice.

"Do you still want to go away?" She was trying.

"Yes, more than ever."

"And your father?"

"He doesn't want me to leave."

"And what will you do if you stay?"

"The store, get married. I don't know. Maybe shit bricks!" It was the first harsh word Jimmy had ever spoken to Dorothy.

"I don't want it that way." She straightened her dress, looked down at it, and was ashamed.

"Neither do I."

"Talk, Jimmy. Please. Talk like you used to talk. Tell me about books, anything."

The words were there, but he had not tried to memorize them while finishing the book earlier in the day. So he remembered the words not knowing how or why he had recalled.

'Let us go gently, gentlemen,' said Don Quixote, 'for there are no birds this year in last year's nest. I was mad, but I am sane now.'

Jimmy finished the words, twisted the ignition and drove the car from the lane. Soon the windows were clear. Jimmy and Dorothy did not speak on their return to Clay Town.

Love On Wheels

"I love you."

"I love you."

"No you don't."

"I do."

"You do not or you'd be here next me." Grover MacFadden touched the empty space which stretched between them. "You'd sit right here." He gently stroked the plastic seat cover.

"Put both hands on the wheel Grover or you'll have us through a ditch. If I've told you once, I've told you ten thousand times, I won't play silly games of sittin' snug, so there."

Grover left off patting the seat and placed his hand on the steering wheel. "All the other guys do it." He pursed his thin, dry lips until the edges were buried in his mouth and only a small shrunken hole remained.

Mary Durance watched the wooden houses pass the window as though she were in a movie house, but the auto was not dark since the sun had climbed to an advantage in the sky. From an interminable distance away it flamed hot lazy rays of afternoon onto the gray metal of the car and onto the upholstery. Then she stopped wiggling in her seat because the houses no longer passed. Only the white steaming ribbon of the highway shot out from beneath the car. She could have watched Slippery Elms, Cedars and Pine Oak lining each side of the narrow road if she had not lowered her head trying to answer Grover MacFadden's sarcasm. She smoothed the hundred folds of her colorful dress.

"I won't because I won't, that's all."

"'Tain't no answer. No other girl in town treats a guy like you do. We've been going together more'n three months..."

"Off an' on," Mary interrupted. "You left me three times to go with Claire Hiker, and I know why."

"Claire ain't got nothing to do with it. Maybe I did get a little necking from her, but it's only because you're so Goddamn Puritan!"

"Puritan is it," she answered watching his calloused hands sweat against the steering wheel. "Just because I'm saving myself for you until after our wedding means nothing. You'd hate me if you knew I had been out with all the boys, wouldn't you? Wouldn't you?"

Grover tightened his grip on the wheel and thought how it would be to rest beside Mary's white skin. He became frightened when he realized he did not like white skin. Embarrassed, he looked at his naked, tan arms and thought about Claire's white patch which had been covered by her bathing suit. In the stern silence, his thoughts returned to the moving auto rolling toward a summer beach on a lake that was closed after August simply because there was nothing to do at a lake in the cold, and because tradition demanded people prepare for winter.

Then his eyes and thoughts were again turned to Mary. He stared at her tanned flats, and he wondered why he had begun to date her. Why was she sitting there beside him when all the time he hated white pure skin and wanted to caress a sun-brown flesh, when he had wanted bodily love and she offered nothing but talk of marriage, and after life, and God. Then he was thinking of his mother, which embarrassed him more because she had pure white skin and he certainly did not want to touch her. Mary acted like his mother, at least the way he thought his mother acted. The car vibrated at sixty miles an hour and the long silence became unbearable.

"I'd like you any way you were," he uttered, wiping the sweat from his broad forehead. "I'd probably like you better if I knew how'd it be after we got married, 'cause a guy's got to try a shoe on to see if it fits."

He wondered why he had not tried this speech on her before. It was an old pitch used by all the other high school boys. Why had he waited until now?

Mary stopped watching the trees and bright green underbrush. "So you compare me to an old shoe is it?"

"I didn't mean that," he said bewildered at her wit.

"Yes you did. You want me like an old shoe so you can throw me away after. If you want a whore for a wife, why then, marry Claire, but me, who's been saving myself after all these years...no better than an old shoe!"

"I didn't mean no such thing."

"Yes you did. You said so." Her gaze returned to the trees outside and the smell of the fields entered strong through the open window.

"The Golding factory is giving us a raise," he said at last. "That will help for the wedding."

"Grover MacFadden, you're changing the subject like you always do. First you want me to be a whore, then you change the subject. There just might'n be a wedding. How much is the raise?"

Grover glanced at her small, girlish face. The long black hair was tied close behind her head then flowed over the seat hanging in a pony tail. Her smooth, soft face glistened in the sun, but he preferred the shadows of her straight nose. She was not pretty. Her thin lips told him that, and all the boys had laughed when he proposed at a party that he, Grover MacFadden, was getting married to Mary Durance. But he cared for something which came with being near her, and he hated himself when he tried to seduce her. He wanted her to be his more than a ring dangling around her neck could do, and he feared and anticipated the night when she would serve herself up to him. She had to give in one day. Even lately she had begun to touch his penis, but when he tried to hug her, she hastily retreated into her father's house.

"We'll get a ten dollar raise a month so that means I'll be clearing $270 a week. That'll give us a good start." He leaned far across the seat and touched her knee.

Mary felt his clumsy pat long after he withdrew the hand, returning his attention to the road. She became frightened in the aftermath, for silence resembled night. The closeness of nature made her aware that they were alone. She could almost reach out and touch the trees — their wildness frightened her even more because they reminded her of Grover who had complete control of her body. He could stop the car and throw her to nature in a sudden fury. She stared at his working hands. It would not do to let him know she was watching just as it would not do to tell him she feared their wedding night because she would lose him forever, into her womanhood. It would be then that they would unite in animal lust in the middle of the orderly underbrush. She knew she loved him. She didn't know why, but she loved him. He must think that she loved his handsome face, which wasn't handsome at all but awkward and animal like. His nose was too large and his broad forehead made such a ridge over his tiny narrow eyes that she thought about him as she thought about a monkey. She hated his thick eyebrows which had grown together on the edge of the brow, and his thick neck made her fear him all the more. She wondered if he was excited and glanced at his two thin shanks then worked her gaze up to his thighs. No, he was concentrating on the road. Besides, it seemed that only night excited THAT in him. She felt close to him but not that close. She feared his body, but she wanted him to suffocate her with love until it hurt. Only then could she feel the pleasure. She wanted to grasp and feel, flowing blood and soft muscle pulsating through, in her, she wanted to use and be used, but she was helplessly caught in her self-inflicted vow to not give in.

Mary turned her gaze to the clouding sky and wished she could have become a nun. Sister Maria Jean had told her more than once that she was fit for the convent, but Mary desired to use and be used, she wanted the pain more. At first she had thought she sinned when thinking about the pleasure-pain. She confessed it to Father Reed, about her impure thoughts, then after she closed her bedroom door and slapped her face until the skin reflected red blotches in the dresser mirror. The thoughts disappeared then, but they returned more frequently, until she became excited with her own body and the pleasure and pain it would offer her when destroyed, the mysterious feeling returned. She once saw herself as a nun in an old book she'd found in the school library. The engraved page depicted a nun bowing to a torture chamber. What amazed Mary was the nun's expression. She was smiling as though she wanted to be tortured. Then there were the pictures of cattle breeding. Mary saw herself bending over as Grover bred her. She had run her fingers through the flame of the gas stove after such a reading.

She forgot about the tortured nun, the animals, the flames when Grover began to kiss her goodnight. At first she wondered what the kiss meant. It was sickly to think of humans kissing like animals, but worse, Grover tried to push his tongue into her mouth. She had to slap him. The nausea which the first open kiss gave to her, disappeared after the first week. Occasionally she allowed him to attempt the "French Kissing" as he explained it, until she became sick after saliva ran onto her new dress. Then she made him stop and just kiss her lightly with his lips.

She wiggled in the seat and watched nature pass.

"You'll look good with a tan," he said. "Every girl should have a tan and go swimming. Why don't you ever want to go?"

"I get burnt," she answered. "No matter what I use for lotion, I look like a lobster. Remember me last summer? I couldn't go out for three whole days."

He laughed and his high pitched voice cut the stiffness of awkward conversation. She again felt the wind on her face. It blew through her hair and the wind felt delightful.

"My little lobster meat," he said. The wind stopped blowing and her cheeks became flushed. "We don't want to get you sun-burned for the wedding. Why don't we just stop at Uncle Sal's farm and walk 'round the fields?"

"I remember what you tried last summer at your uncle's farm when we were just dating."

She opened the small air vent. The breeze had stopped, but they were traveling at sixty miles an hour. Her cheeks became more flushed and Grover's knuckles were red from gripping the steering wheel so tightly. Trees peered down at her from the hills and she feared them.

"That was last summer. It's gone by so why not try fighting me 'gain. 'Tain't nothing wrong with talking and walking through fields with the girl you're gonna marry."

Grover was planning the walk already. They would follow the cow path until the little field opened beneath the clump of trees, and he would carry a blanket this time. That was what prevented her giving in last year. He almost had her then. Was that the reason he had insisted on driving this road to the beach? He satisfied himself that such thoughts had never entered his mind.

"You can stop if the feeling's got you," she answered after some silence. Wild bunches of speckled and white and yellow daisies passed her window. She wanted to reach out and gather a handful of stems.

"Might we pick some flowers?" she asked.

"If you want flowers I'll pick these hills clean," Grover answered.

She saw the real child-man emerge from the animal body. Now he was being sweet. Mary knew he had said it to entice her into the fields, but she forgave him.

"Sure 'tis a wonder you're not a Longfellow," she said in her Irish brogue she used when feeling full of humor.

"And you, me colleen," he answered. Yes, this was the Grover MacFadden who she yearned to live with. Now the beast had been drowned with light-hearted humor. The beast was waiting in the field.

"Now you promise just to walk and pick flowers?"

Grover knew she was jesting. Her insistence angered him. Why couldn't she be like other girls who liked necking and petting? He decided to approach her with the argument, partially because her persistence angered him, partially because he took delight in knowing that she was different from the rest.

"'Bout time you got a job?" he asked. "The wedding is almost here and you just hole up at home like you was a hot house plant."

"You know well and good that I'm not about to work." Her voice was soft but deliberate. "I won't be running around in overhauls and T-shirts like your other girl friends."

"They're all working," he continued. "Nancy's at the bank. Claire's a waitress. Peg's helping her ol' man, and even Elsa is washing dishes at Mike's Steak House. Ain't no reason for you not to get a little job to give us pin money."

"We've been through this before." Mary folded her arms and slumped in the seat. "I won't work. I won't work."

"What if I get laid off and we have ten children and the house is going to be taken away from us and we ain't got our parents to help? Would you work then?"

"The woman's place is in the house," Mary spoke with finality.

"But we ain't got a home yet?"

"We'll have one if you're at all serious about marrying me. You said we could move straight into the Brunson place. I can fix it up like your own home. I'm telling you again, my place is in the home."

"Jesus Christ, Mary, the city's full of girls who got jobs. It's the thing to do. Why in a few years the women will be supporting husbands!"

"Then in a few years this country will go to the devil. And if you want to compare me with those bad girls, why, I'd just as soon you stop the car and let me walk home!"

"Things will be tough," Grover said nearing the end of the argument. "When we have the first kid he ain't gonna have benefits like others."

Mary felt happy even if, in the near future, she had to submit herself beneath the clawing appetite of Grover MacFadden. From the pain comes the joy and the baby would be lasting and not pass in a moment. She could hold it. The infant wouldn't claw.

"Grover! Stop at that billboard!" she demanded.

"Why?"

"'Cause it looks funny, that's all."

The car rocked over the edge of the pavement and slid through the gravel. A thin coat of dust was settling over the car as Mary walked toward the sign. Through the dust, Grover caught up with her.

"What's so funny 'bout an old sign post?" he asked. "It ain't even got a picture on it."

"But look at the cracks," she said. "They look like that modern art Mr. Jaffers showed us in art class."

"You always did eat that stuff up," he said sticking his hands up to the knuckles in his khaki pockets.

"Look here," she said pointing to a hole in the sign. "This is the moon, no, the sun, and these lines leading away from it are people's lives. See how tiny they are. They go to the bottom of the sign then they return to the sun. The slashes through the lines stand for pain."

"There's a helleva lot of slashes if you ask me," Grover said disinterested in art.

"They are beautiful because for each slash the lines go on."

"Yeah, but they go to the bottom. They ain't like life."

"But they return to the sun, don't they?" she asked.

Grover turned the car onto a steep, unpaved road at the familiar turn. The road twisted, turned, climbed, descended, then climbed again until they passed along sharp ridges above the patched green and brown of autumn farm lands. Small farm houses were dwarfed by large barns. Some stood alone on knolls far from the weaving road. Others, similar to doll houses, were wedged between hills, slumbering deep in valleys. Cows lumbered beside rusty fences. They peered disinterested toward the rolling wheels. Almost at each turn in the road there was a herd of cows and work horses grazing on the steep slopes. The roar of the engine broke their hilltop tranquility, but the only objection the animals demonstrated was raising their heads and watching the auto pass.

"Poor people live in them houses," Grover said watching the road. "There ain't one new car in them garages."

"Since when were people poor when they didn't feel like buying a new car each year?" Mary asked. "These people are probably better put than your father."

"They're not. They're poor!" Grover exclaimed because he

knew them. "Uncle Sal showed me 'round and lots of 'em ain't even got TVs." Mary laughed.

"Well, they don't. And they have to cut their wood for fires to keep warm."

"Are they any different than the Stucko's in town?" Mary asked. "Or the Davies, or the Peaks?"

"They ain't that poor."

"Yes they are," Mary continued. "They're probably much poorer in money, but these people are happy. Now admit they're not happy?"

"You're right," he gave in. "They're happy 'cause they don't know the outside like we do. They got sex and that's all that counts, huh?"

"Must you bring that into every sentence?" she asked. Her face became crimson.

Grover wiggled in the seat. He was not sorry he had said the word. He reached across the seat to comfort her, but his effort ended in a slap across the fingers. He jerked his hand to the wheel and drove on in silence.

"Don't you like sex? Don't you like me?" he asked. "Don't you, huh? Don't you?"

The beast was loose again. Mary became frightened. She knew that when it came, the shock would be great. The first plunge would be deep and hard because she had never controlled IT, never allowed IT to have small satisfactions. She held onto the door handle while speaking.

"Can't you wait a couple of more months until our wedding? I know it's hard but we have waited so long and it means so much to me. Please wait and trust?"

"But I can't wait!" he almost shouted. "You are there beneath your dress and I want you! You're mine and I want you!"

Mary reached across the empty space and held his hand tightly. She felt the blood pulsating against her palm. She knew he was too excited to be calmed by talk. She was silent for a moment.

"Grover, you can't. I'm in my period." It was a lie and she hated herself as much as she hated his trembling body.

"I will, by God! I will! We're almost to Uncle Sal's and then I will. I will have you, or by Jesus, I'll rape you!"

She withdrew her hand and put it against her mouth. It would be impossible to stop him once he held her skin against his. She dropped her hand onto her lap and became calm. Her body grew limp. "Grover?"

"No! Don't try to talk me out of it!"

"I won't," she answered meekly. "But you promised me daisies. There's a bunch up there along the road. Please pick me some?"

"We can wait till we get there. It's only a mile or so."

"I want them now. Don't you love me at all? Please? Just a few. We can smell them together, before..."

He stopped the car, slipped from the seat and slammed the door. While he bent to pick the flowers, Mary slipped behind the wheel, engaged the engine and left him standing on the roadside.

"He will thank me after our wedding," she thought driving back to town by another route.

The dust left from the auto rested gently on his shoulders. A bee perched on the picked daisies in his hand and still he did not move. He felt anger and hatred, but mostly disappointment. His heart sank until the blood flowed normally through his veins. And still he held the daisies looking after the car in silence.

Only when the roar of the engine was out of hearing did

he look down at the flowers. They were ugly and wilted. The sun stroked his face and arms. The smell of manure entered his nostrils, and his feet sank deeper and deeper into the soft earth. He became embellished with nature. He felt a large well of un-expanded energy fill his limbs. He knew he must do something, yell, fly, throw himself into the grass, cry, pray! The bee flew away. A moment later he ran over the small knoll and down into the valley toward his uncle's farm. The meadow grass was high and dry. His feet cut the weeds with their speed. He saw the patch of trees in which he had planned to take Mary. He plunged headlong into their thickness. He screamed and his voice echoed through the valley.

Return

Four young men, all the age of army induction, sat around a large oil drum, open on the top for burning trash, or rather, three sat on the soft September dirt and one sprawled, leaning on his elbows. Dody Blake rolled over and stared at the ground. "Christ, it's just getting dark and nobody'll be there."

The three youths watched the flames leap from the barrel.

"Now don't be backing out, Larry. It was your idea!"

"We could get bit sitting back here like this." Larry McBridy looked about him.

"Bit by what?" Dody picked up a discarded nylon stocking and inspected it.

"By rats, that's what! This place is full of 'em."

"Sure rats! Two legged ones." Dody was pleased with his remark and approved the joke by laughing.

"Larry's right, Dody. It's not healthy sittin' out here." Paul Steiner was scared.

"Let's go in then."

"If you're so brave, why ain't you gone in?" Grover MacFadden slapped Dody's leg playfully. "You just go in and we'll follow. Won't we follow?"

"Look," Dody exclaimed pointing toward the large gray wooden house. "It's just a whore house. Lot's of guys go in there at night and nothing bites them. Nobody's gonna see ya. Nobody's there. I bet they don't even have women on call."

"Then why should we go in?"

"'Cause we got a bet. Now, Larry said, 'let's go to the whore house this morning', and so here we are. You game or ain't ya?"

"Look, I don't have no money." Grover turned his pockets inside out. "No money, no girls."

"I only got ten dollars!" Paul Steiner stared at the white pockets hanging like parched tongues. "So how can we get girls if we don't have enough money?"

"Let's divvy up and just see."

Dody dug deep into his pockets and came up with two ten dollar bills and a handful of change. Paul Steiner contributed his ten dollars. Larry McBridy threw five dollars onto the pile.

"Well, this is different." Dody counted the money. "With my change it comes to $36 dollars. Now it takes twenty apiece, so I hear. Let's draw lots and see who goes."

"You and Grover go on," Paul said rising to his feet. "I'd just rather not."

"Me too," Larry McBridy said following Paul out of the backyard.

"You guys ain't scared, are ya?" Dody yelled.

"Not us, we're just giving you the fun."

"Sure, sure, we know, fun. We'll tell you 'bout it later."

Grover MacFadden watched until they disappeared down the alley then he turned to Dody. "You really gonna try it?"

"We got thirty-six dollars, ain't we?"

They walked quickly and quietly to the back door and rang the bell. Soon the heavy door opened slightly.

"What do you kids want?"

Dody was frightened. He wanted to run, but Grover was near him. Paul and Larry would find out. He could not speak.

"We want in, what do you think?"

"We're closed."

"Look, we're old 'nuff, and this place ain't closed 'cause I know." Grover felt courage dominate over fear since anger had replaced it. Anger was motivated by anyone who thought him a child.

Doris Gray stood behind the door not allowing the youths to see her. Oh, what the hell, everybody in this town knew except her, and now she knows, so why not. But then Doris thought about Betty, her recently returned daughter. Teen-agers never came to the house, only old, calloused men, thin men, and not pleasant men, men terrible to touch, men from the trains. Why had they come now with their young soft skin? Had they known that she was coming?

"We're closed."

"Momma, let them in!" The young voice came from inside the large house, but it was closer before it was again heard. "Momma, aren't you running a business here? I've got to prove myself, don't I?"

"No! You're leaving!" Doris turned to give final instructions to the voice, but the source was past her. The door swung wide.

"Hi! Don't mind Momma, she just don't like young fellows, but I do. Come in, come in. We don't have no one around but the two of us. The old matron and her yearling."

The girl led them through the dim high passage. She wore a a bright yellow cotton dress and bounced gaily in front of them. Her black hair swayed from side to side.

"She sure is dressed up to be here, huh, Grover?"

Dody's friend did not have a chance to answer. She beckoned them to enter into a well lighted, pink painted room housing three couches, a table beside a large cash register, another low table covered with magazines, and a small bar half hidden by the third couch where Mrs. Gray had retreated. The girl led them into this reception room. The faded pink and smell of cheap perfume almost made Dody sick. He wanted to run, anywhere

— upstairs, over barrels, — he stumbled behind the young girl, giddy and light headed. Soon he began to laugh.

"Do we take our clothes off here?" he asked knowing it was a stupid question, but not caring.

Doris felt sorry for the youths who were obviously entering for the first time. "Betty! We're closed!"

"But Momma? I just got here!" Betty ran to a suitcase as if to prove her remark.

"They all call me momma," Doris said. "Being a matron gives them the idea that I'm motherly." Doris poured herself another drink.

"My God," Grover spoke, noticing the girl who had led them into the room. "She's no older'n us."

"But I've been around, haven't I, Momma?"

"Don't call me Momma!" Doris was angry.

"But Momma, why did you write Cleveland if you didn't want me? Now we have customers. Nice looking ones too. Isn't it a shame the others aren't here to see such beautiful masculine forms, huh, Momma?"

Grover took off his cap and stared. Dody sat on the couch. Betty ran and jumped onto his lap. "Oh my goodness, isn't this one bashful, she shouted with glee, bouncing on Dody's knees. "But Momma, he sure is excited!" The girl began to giggle.

Doris raised her head high and breathed through her nose then walked to the cash register. Not looking down, she stumbled against a chair but managed to pull herself straight.

"The money, gentlemen, please?"

"But Momma, they don't have to pay until we've gone to bed, now isn't that the way all the houses work, at least it was that way in Cleveland."

"Yes dear," Doris caught herself. "Yes Betty, they can pay now or later."

"Later Momma. Let them pay later." Betty jumped up and

down. "You know, Momma, that way they have a nice tip when they've been to bed with me. Well, who's first?" She poised her index finger to her lips then pointed toward Gover.

"I like him. Don't you, Momma?"

"Please Betty, tell them we're closed." Doris was busying herself at the register.

"But this one here is so excited!" Betty felt Dody's forehead.

"You mean that both of us are going to lay you?"

Grover watched her fast movements and became hypnotized by her staccato voice.

"And why not? I'm a girl and I love all you big masculine men."

"Me first!" Dody shouted. "She said so, huh Betty?"

"What do you think, Momma?"

"Please, please, no more of this. It isn't right, Betty. Must you torture me?" The two boys stared at the heavy woman. Her shoulders heaved strongly.

"Momma is jealous 'cause I came back to take her business away from her." Betty threw her long black hair back and laughed loudly. She crossed her legs and gathered the cotton dress around her waist. "You see, gentlemen, I just arrived from Cleveland where she thought I was in a girl's school, but they have houses there too. Little did I know it was in my blood."

"Stop you whore!" Doris shouted and rushed toward Betty. She slapped the child across the chin. Betty laughed as the red marks began to show color. "You are going this minute!"

"But Matron, I just answered your ad. I've been gone from Clay Town ever so long that I didn't hardly remember your number until I saw it on our bulletin board. I only knew your home number, never your business number. But now I know. Sir? Are you coming up with me?" She took Dody by the hand and he followed her willingly.

90

The upstairs door slammed before Doris raised her head and noticed Grover watching her.

"Something wrong, ma'am?"

"Mind your own business!" Doris looked at her hands, and they were hard.

Grover seized a magazine with a red and yellow cover displaying women in brief clothing. He resigned his body to the wait but his mind was puzzling. The pictures passed — nude, inviting — but his thoughts rebounded to the big National Cash Register and the heavy woman. Betty had been rude, but why? Minutes passed and he noticed the sweat beads melt trenches through the woman's heavy make-up.

"You want I go with you?" Grover decided to sacrifice.

"Shut up! Goddamn you, shut up!" Doris saw the red enter around her knuckles as she pressed against the chair.

"I just thought maybe, well, maybe you was hurt 'cause the girl is young and pretty and..."

"Thanks." Doris bowed her head and stopped seeing the pink of the room or the red of her knuckles.

"There ain't no call to feel that she's any better than you 'cause, 'cause..." Grover stopped.

Mrs. Gray was sobbing. Suddenly the door opened above them and heavy steps began to descend the stairs. Startled, Grover and Mrs. Gray looked upward. Dody, cap in hand, stiffened each leg before it hit the lower step. At the bottom he stopped and scratched his head.

"My God, you've only been up there a few minutes?" Grover was more puzzled.

"She won't stop crying! Just lays there and she won't stop crying long 'nuff." Dody was ashamed and hurt. It must be my fault, he thought, but what did he do wrong? He had been so careful.

Mrs. Gray, alive for the first time in minutes, started for the stairs. She climbed slowly at first then pulled her gown high and ran upward.

"Betty! My child, my child! Why did you have to find out? Why, why, Why?" she repeated on each step. Then she disappeared into the room and the boys, hearing the confession, stood silently staring at the large cash register. Finally, Grover spoke their thoughts, "Let's get out of here."

They ran through the alley, shaded by twilight, jumping imaginary puddles, pushing over garbage cans, hitting parked cars. Grover was the first to feel exhaustion. He slumped to the pebbles and dirt in front of a garage. Dody ran on for a few yards, stopped, and walked back to Grover. He squatted to hear his friend.

"What we gonna tell 'em?"

"Give 'em the money and tell 'em to go to hell! It was closed."

"Sure, closed." Grover tossed a pebble at the garage window across the sea of dirty oil. "Hey, let's do something real big tonight."

"Like what?" Dody shoved the cap on the crown of his head.

"Don't know. Race maybe?"

"Let's get drunk! That's what I say!" Dody produced a fifth of whiskey from beneath his shirt. Grover had been in too much of a hurry to notice.

"Why'd you do that for?"

"They won't be needin' it. If they're what I think they are..."

"Let's find Paul and Larry. They got a right to the whiskey too." Grover was again on his feet. Dody quickly followed and hit Grover in the arm.

"Sure, we'll find 'em and have a helleva time. But she was sure good looking to be that kind, huh Grover?"

The two young men labored down the alley. Dody took a drink and handed the bottle to Grover. Darkness hid their shadows as they turned onto Grant Street.

Pickup

Jinny Pin stood on High School Hill and peered out toward the town below. Groups of children ran from house to house carrying bags. It was Halloween, but few were in costume. Only the large trees, lining the cracked and patched streets seemed to celebrate the event as their changed colors signaled the advent of winter.

The two block long business district along Grant Street was deserted. The stillness reminded Jinny of the play, Brigadoon. Then she remembered it was dinner time.

The stately high school, directly below, commanded an impressive height on the largest hill surrounding the town.

Jinny thought about her four years behind those walls. They sped past in her memory. Forty seconds for four years, ten seconds a year: the day she loaned her handkerchief to Billy Pango because he had forgotten his, the polished oak floor of the long hall, the excited note Harry O'Brien had passed, and Mr. Crawly, the science teacher, who she secretly loved over the span of three and one half years until he moved back to the city somewhere in Pennsylvania. Jinny had never inquired where.

Jinny felt comfortable on the spot where she could gaze at her inheritance: the stores, the churches, the offices, the bars, the homes. But she could not remain long before a sense of despair and futility overcame her. She turned away from the cool breeze and the hidden five thousand residents.

The path led over the hill. She had walked it hundreds of times. She knew every fork, one leading to Plant #3, another to the old almost forgotten Catholic cemetery. This evening she chose the path which would eventually direct her down the hill to the Westway. Harry O'Brien would be stopping for a drink before turning in his mail bag for the day.

His wife's death had forced Harry to drink too much. Many an evening Jinny stood at her office window and watched the lone figure stagger past, pulling himself toward an empty evening.

Jinny quickened her pace along the dirt path. She ignored the exploding autumn colors around her. Nature was at work, within and without.

Jinny walked nervously into the bar. She had never stepped inside before. Not knowing what to do, she approached the counter and stood next to Harry O'Brien. His mail satchel sat limp on the barroom floor as he sipped a beer.

Jinny was not aware that Paul Steiner watched her enter as he played the pin ball machine.

"Jinny Pin! What are you doing here?" Harry asked recognizing his once schoolmate in the mirror. "Happy Halloween!"

Nervously Jinny looked for the bartender, not wanting him to appear.

"Mother wanted some ale. She drinks a tiny glass every evening before she goes to bed."

Jinny measured an imaginary short glass with her fingers.

"You should get it at the liquor store," Harry replied. "Beer, excuse me, ale is pretty expensive here."

"The liquor store is closed at this hour."

"No 'tain't," Hank Stark, the bartender, volunteered as he approached the two.

"Sure it is! It's Halloween," Harry O'Brien defended Jinny's decision to visit the bar. He pushed closer to the female standing next to him at the counter.

"Did you hear that the Ottoman plant is shutting down? Guess they're moving south like all the rest."

"That's terrible!" Jinny replied. "What's to become of this town?"

"Good riddance to sour milk, that's what I say," the bartender offered.

"Them factories can't pay their way. Been a burden on the town since the thirties. Kept the railroad from makin' this a real town."

"Not so, and you know it, Hank," Harry picked up his glass and stared at it as if reading a crystal ball.

"The railroad shops moved out in the thirties because of the strike. President of the railroad swore he'd make grass grow on the streets of this town. Sewer pipe factories been the only thing keepin' us going."

"The sidewalks are a disgrace," Jinny injected. "They're so cracked and uneven no one can walk on them."

"Blame the unions," Harry responded.

"Unions hell!" Hank rejoined. "You can blame the mayor and his tribe! Jinny? How many ale's you want?"

The question caught Jinny by surprise. She had forgotten her embarrassment during the heat of the conversation. Now she quickly stepped back from the bar as if separating herself from a contaminating experience.

All activity stopped while everyone present stared at her.

"Just one, thank you. I'll stop at the grocery tomorrow. I was just passing and thought it would be easier to buy it here."

"Got to charge a dollar."

"I'll pay for it," Harry offered throwing a dollar bill onto the counter. "And give Jinny a Cherry. It'll do her good."

"Cherry?" Jinny asked.

Harry gently led Jinny to a table near the pin ball machine. "Bring it over to the table. Jinny's going to tip a glass with her old schoolmate."

"I had better start home. Mother will be wondering." Jinny made no effort to collect the paper bag which contained the ale. She allowed Harry to direct her toward the table.

She stopped at the pin ball machine as Harry took a seat at the booth. "Paul Steiner!" she exclaimed. "What are you doing here?"

"I came in to play a couple of games and racked up fifty ."

"I hope you're not taking to drink?"

"Hardly, Miss Pin. I just like to watch the people."

"Come on over, Jinny and taste some good Cherry!" the mailman spoke from the booth.

"Good night, Paul."

Paul turned to the machine plunger with some embarrassment.

"Good night, Miss Pin."

Jinny scooted onto the booth seat.

"They're growing up. I used to babysit Paul Steiner when he was no higher than the Fourth of July corn."

"Try your Cherry?" Harry asked.

Jinny sipped and nodded her approval. It was an awkward moment in their newly found adult relationship. Jinny should have said something about the drink. Her approving nod left Harry groping for words, phrases, paragraphs to bridge the expanse of two human beings wanting to lie together in the gentle grass of nature.

"What do you think will become of us?" Jinny asked after another sip. The Cherry had warmed her tongue.

"Us?"

"The town." Jinny realized her double meaning.

"What will happen when the clay factories are all gone? It's our only industry."

"Not so," Harry felt on solid ground again. "There's the Grimes Slaughter House and the Steiner boats."

"That's hardly enough to keep five thousand people from starving."

"We'll become a bedroom community for the big towns around us."

"Heavens, Harry! They are thirty and forty miles away!"

"That's nothing for city people to drive, and they can take the train to Columbus."

"Why would they want to live here?" Jinny asked between sips.

"Cities are cesspools. People want to get away. Did you know they have designated this town as an evacuation area in case the cities get blown up?"

They talked through three beers and two Cherries. Not all was adult bantering. They slipped easily into reminiscing about high school days: the time Harry wore a suit to be different and changed the style of everyday jeans, the time Billy Pango stuck Jinny in the arm with a pencil and she worried about contracting lead poisoning, and about the prom when Harry got so drunk he vomited in the back seat, and his date, Julie Terrance, whom he later married, would not talk to him for a month. Now she was dead, killed in a car crash.

They found themselves on the dark street discussing the fate of classmates, but the subject of Julie was eclipsed.

Harry swung the mail satchel which held the bottle of ale. In a flood of giggling repartee, Jinny had entrusted the purchase to Harry as she once did with her take-home school books.

Jinny touched each familiar light post in order to keep herself steady and fixed in reality.

A block from Jinny's house the question was asked. Harry stopped and stared into her eyes.

"Would you like to come to my house for a glass of milk or something?" Harry impulsively reached for her hand.

Jinny broke away and stepped back into the shadows. "What do you think I am, Harry O'Brien? A pickup?" She turned and fled in the direction of her house. Harry did not realize he was carrying Jinny's bottle of ale until he reached his own door...

Dag carried his second bag of trick or treats down Third Street stopping at each lighted house. He wore the High Hat from his Uncle Sam's uniform, which he waved leading the Clay Day Parade each summer.

The other bag of treats was stashed in a garbage can behind the bakery on Grant Street waiting for Dag to claim it and head home, hopefully with a free ride from the sheriff or West Clay Town resident.

He walked to the lighted house and rang the bell. Harry O'Brien opened the door.

Dag held out his bag. "Har! tick or treat!"

"You're too old to be doing this Dag. Go away."

"I'm Uncle Sam," Dag answered with hope.

"Then write me a check!" Harry sneered.

"Check? Har! Got no check. Bag for candy."

Harry removed his wallet. "Here's five dollars. Leave me alone, or I'll call the police."

"No want police be bad. Be good. Go home to Mousie. Happy." Dag forgot the occasion. "Happy happy."

"Go home, Dag. Enough!"

Dag bowed and tipped his high hat. The door closed and he was alone.

"Go home to Mousie with supply of candy," Dag muttered to himself. "He no yell at Dagbert."

He ran back to Grant Street and approached the waste can which lay on its side, the lid a few feet away. "Much candy for Mousie and me." Dag lifted the trash can and reached in for his resources. There was nothing there. He picked up pieces of torn paper nearby.

"Dog get candy." The hard earned chocolate was lost forever.

Dag lowered his head and walked home with one half filled bag of chocolates and a five dollar bill. It was not all lost.

Part III

WINTER

Early Death

"You're scared!"

"I'm not!"

"Yes you are!"

"I'm here ain't I?"

Larry McBridy swung one rubber covered leg over the fence then sat straddling the wood. Allowing his body to relax, he stared down at his fourteen year old brother.

"You don't even know how to carry a shot gun! Christ, Jimmy, you could blow yourself up leaning on a gun that way!"

Young Jimmy McBridy pushed the 410 gage shot gun away from his stocky body. Larry, sitting on the fence as if it were a young colt, fastening the heels of his hip boots onto one of the rungs, shook his head.

"You don't have a toy now, Jimmy. For Christ-sakes, hold that thing like I taught you."

"I'm tired."

"Do as I told you!"

Jimmy raised the gun by its stock and held the loading chamber against his chest with the barrel pointing toward the light gray winter sky.

"That's better," Larry said resting the stock of his 16 gage shot gun firmly on his right thigh.

"Never hold the barrel toward you, unless you want to kill yourself."

Larry reached into the pocket of the brown canvas hunting coat and pulled out a stick of chewing tobacco. He bit off a piece of the coal-black bar, which he held in his left hand still grasping the gun with his right. The barrel cast sun rays across the trees behind them. Chewing, then spitting once, Larry looked calmly into the open field on the other side of the fence.

"You'd catch it if father knew that you chewed," Jimmy said examining the open breech of his gun.

"You'd better not tell him or I won't bring you hunting no more. I like to chew when I'm hunting, that's all."

"You never chew when you're with father, I bet," Jimmy said.

"That's all you know. He just might never had said nothing 'cause mother was always around when we got back, and he didn't want to cause no trouble. You just don't know?"

"Then I can tell Mom, can't I?" Jimmy asked leaning a polished boot on the first rung of the fence.

"You'd just better not or I won't bring you no more. You're a momma's boy, and you don't have no right out here. So I just might make this the first and last time I bring you hunting."

"You'd better not!" Jimmy removed his boot from the fence and kicked at the frozen earth.

"You promised me that we'd go hunting often when I got my own gun, and now I got one so please don't be mean. Nobody's gonna teach me if you don't." He wiped his boots carefully with his hand, careful to keep the gun barrel pointed upward.

"I'm grown up now."

"You're not and you know it," Larry said. "Just because father bought you a gun for Christmas don't mean you're a hunter. You got to kill something to prove that. And you're not gonna kill nothing if you stand here sniffing away 'bout me chewing!"

"Let's go then," Jimmy said climbing the fence.

"Christ, Jimmy! I tell you something one minute and you forget it the next."

Jimmy stopped climbing the fence.

"What's wrong?"

"Don't point that barrel at me! Don't point that barrel at nobody!"

"Gee, I'm sorry, Larry. I forgot." Jimmy raised the long steel into the December sky. "But how can I climb a fence holding my gun like this?"

"I got my gun raised don't I?"

"But you're bigger'n me," Jimmy spoke not daring to move.

"Yeah, and I'm four years older than you so you'd better listen and learn the first time."

"You just tell me how to get over this fence with my gun and I'll do just what you say."

"That's easy. Put the gun against it." Larry spit allowing the stillness to settle around them. "Climb over, then reach across and get it."

"Gee, that's simple," Jimmy responded by leaning the gun against the fence and scurrying over. He reached over the top rung and pulled the gun to him. He followed Larry, holding the gun tightly against his chest. His brother leaned far over the other side, spit, then reached for the fence.

"You got the hang of it now." Larry swung the other foot over the wood, balanced his bottom then shoved his body forward with both feet. Holding the gun in his right hand, Larry landed next to his brother.

"Gee, you're awful good at that, Larry."

"It takes practice. Fence climbing and walking through underbrush is important to hunting, but the main thing is the kill. You got to aim straight and pull the trigger sure and quick. A rabbit won't wait around all day for you."

Jimmy felt the blood rush to his head. He hoped Larry

would not notice his red face, but everyone did notice it. When the boys in his ninth grade class asked him to play football at recess, and he had blushed, they noticed it, or when his father had asked him to help clean a dead fish, Jimmy couldn't stop the blood from rushing into his face, and his father would turn away and ask Larry to apply the knife. Larry did not notice the redness now. His brother walked past him without noticing, and Jimmy could smell the stink of chewing tobacco and the odor of dead rabbits from his brother's coat. He felt like dying or, at least, excusing himself and running away. He had excused himself before. That time last summer when his father and Larry had taken him along to shoot rats at the city dump. He had walked over to the edge of the garbage-filled dump and looked down. The smoldering smoke and stink of rotten things had filled his nostrils. Suddenly, without warning, the foot-long rat had run across his shoe. Jimmy felt himself beating against the soft body of the rat with the baseball bat he carried in the left hand, his father and Larry shouting for him to stop, that the rat was dead, but Jimmy could not stop smashing the spongy flesh of the rat until his father seized the ball bat and drove him back home in the car. Greeting his mother, Jimmy had excused himself with tears and vomit.

Following the hip boots of his brother across the hard chunks of earth, stumbling at each step, Jimmy knew he could not excuse himself this time. He had read it in that novel, and then his father had said it to his mother. Puberty. It was there, in the thick pages of his brother's dictionary. "The age of puberty is", then the word, adult entered his thoughts. Larry had said it before he asked for the gun...

"Christ Jimmy," Larry had shouted after coming home from fall football practice. "You got to grow up sometime. You got to prove yourself. You got to stop hanging around the house behind mom's skirts and act like father and me. You got to go hunting and fishing and take a liking for them kind of games."

Then his father had said it secretly to his mother. "Jimmy's getting along toward being a man. It's 'bout time isn't it, Martha?" And the answer was a whispered, yes.

He couldn't excuse himself now. He stopped and admired the stiff brown material of the hunting jacket. He feared the time when the pockets, extending around the bottom of the coat, would be filled with the kill. First the gun for Christmas and then yesterday, when he had opened the birthday package, he knew there must be no more excuses. Never again did he want his father to turn away from him and call Larry. He wanted to find his father like he had been yesterday.

"Well Jimmy, want to try out your new gun and coat tomorrow?"

The blood had not rushed to Jimmy's head. He was too proud and happy. He only smiled when his father turned to Larry.

"Larry, you want to take your brother out tomorrow? I've got some work to do."

Then the moment arrived as Jimmy looked at the tall lanky frame of his brother, Larry, the sportsman, the football star, the high school personality. Larry nodded.

A bird winged into the sky from a clump of bushes. The sound of flapping wings against the cold air brought the blood to Jimmy's face.

"You still with me?" his brother asked turning to look at the small boy. "You scared, Jimmy?" His brother had seen.

"Gee, no. No, I ain't scared. Why should I be scared of a bird or a rabbit?"

"That's right," Larry said. "There isn't a thing to be scared of." He spit.

Jimmy stared at the brown puddle of saliva marking the frozen ground.

"We might not even see a rabbit today." Larry knew. "And even if we do, they're so small that they can't hurt you."

"How does it feel, Larry?"

"How does what feel?"

"The kill?"

Larry laughed. The laughter echoed across the field. Then he lowered his voice and squinted. "There's nothing like it. That's the real thrill of hunting. Remember the time I got our car going a hundred and ten miles an hour?"

"Sure. I was scared then."

"Naw, you weren't really scared. That was a thrill. And the kill is a lot more thrilling than that!"

"I was scared, Larry." Jimmy lowered the gun.

"It's because you weren't grown up. Christ sakes, watch that gun! You'll end up killing me! It may only be a 410, but I don't want no doctor picking buckshot out of my ass."

It was Jimmy's turn to laugh, and the echoes, hollow and vibrating, frightened him, but he could not stop.

"Be quiet." Larry commanded. "You're going to scare away all the rabbits."

"Maybe there ain't none here, Larry? Maybe they all left? It's too cold for 'em to leave their holes. I heard that snakes don't leave their holes all winter."

"I told you that, stupe. But rabbits like to run when it's cold. They got to eat, don't they?"

"What do snakes eat if they never come out of their holes all winter?" Jimmy asked.

"They hibernate like bears. Come on, we got to get to the hollow before we'll see any rabbits."

"It's pretty cold out here. Gee, it was nice and warm in bed this morning."

Larry turned quickly and heaved his gun over the padded right shoulder.

"Do you want to go home?" he shouted.

"No, I was just thinking how cold it is here. I bet you're cold in them rubber boots?" Jimmy asked, trying to change the anger he recognized in Larry.

"They're insulated and plenty warm. Now come on. We got to get home for dinner and we'll never shoot a rabbit before then if we keep on gabbing. And put a shell in that gun. I didn't know you were carrying it empty. You've got to load it the minute you get on the field. Now put three shells in."

Larry spit again and walked away from Jimmy. The small boy stared at the second puddle of saliva. It did not make him sick even though he could smell the juice. The dead rat had made him sick, or was it the presence of the rat before he killed it? No, he had become sick by touching the scales of that bluegill, but that was so long ago, and the fish was flopping, so maybe he got sick when tiny things were alive, knowing he had to kill them.

Jimmy lowered the gun and stared into the long barrel. He saw only a black hole, but he knew what would be in there, deep in the hole, ready to come charging out with a slight jerk of the trigger. He reached into the deep pocket and pulled out three shells. He slipped them into the breech and closed it. Then he swung the gun over his right shoulder imitating Larry. He had to run a few yards to catch up with his brother.

They walked into the shadows of the hollow. The two boys had walked beneath the sun while crossing the field, but now they left it resting on the top of a hill. Larry lunged through the thick underbrush even though there was an opening to the right of it. Jimmy hesitated, kicked at the dry weeds and walked around to the path leading into the cluster of trees which formed the hollow. He had been here before, but without a gun resting on his shoulder. On those early visits he liked the coolness offered by the large trees. He liked the closeness of the trees while running with his friends along the path leading through the hollow with a small creek cutting through the middle of it. On those summer afternoons, it had been fun to enter the hollow carrying empty whiskey bottles found along the road which they threw into the creek. He always enjoyed throwing stones at the floating bottles even if he never hit any. Now he entered slowly, tramping softly on the twigs which broke beneath his feet. Larry stopped.

"Wait a minute," he said disappearing behind a thick vine-covered elm tree. Jimmy stared at the fat barrel of the 16 gage shot gun which Larry had leaned against the tree. Somehow it was warmer in here. The wind had stopped, but his feet felt numb.

"Come on! Come on!" Larry whispered taking up his gun and plunging farther into the heart of the hollow in the direction of the creek. I'm giving you the first shot," Larry whispered when Jimmy caught up to him.

"What if I miss?"

"Then I'll get it. My gun's better at long range, and besides, I want you to show father that you got your kill the very first day. Now be quiet and walk alongside me. I know there's plenty of 'em in here." They hadn't walked three steps before the bushes rustled ten feet to Jimmy's left. Larry shouted into his right ear.

"Kill him! Kill him! He'll come right into the clearing there, in front of us. For Christ sakes, follow him with your gun!"

Jimmy obeyed the command, jerking the stock of the gun firmly against his shoulder and pointing the barrel at the moving weeds. He aimed the gun slowly following the weeds as the unseen rabbit moved toward them. The blood rushed into his head, and he felt his finger freeze on the trigger. The rabbit might never appear. He felt sick. The barrel became heavy, forcing his arm muscles to lower it slightly. Then the white running fur was passing before the barrel and into the clearing. Larry shouted something. The trees and vines behind the bounding rabbit blurred. Jimmy saw water. He felt the world explode. He saw branches. His shoulder hurt and his ears were ringing. Suddenly he was reclining on soft grass. A stream of sun invaded the hollow through trees overhead, shimmering on the gun barrel. Jimmy knew there was nothing inside now to vomit forward in tiny pellets. He hadn't stopped shooting until all three shells had been discharged.

"You got the kill. Christ alive, my little brother got his first one!" Larry shouted and danced around Jimmy.

"I didn't think you had it in you, but you did it!"

Larry leaned his gun against a tree, spit, and disappeared. Jimmy could not take his eyes away from the barrel. Smoke seemed to crawl from the black hole. Then he did look up, Larry was standing over him holding the rabbit by the hind feet. Larry shook his extended arm and the animal danced.

"Is he dead?" Jimmy asked from the soft grass. The leaves were wet against his head, but they felt good.

"Sure as shooting! You peppered him with that 410. He sure met death early though." Larry said shaking the rabbit.

"What do you mean?"

"Oh, nothing, 'cept he's pretty young. Look how small. But don't worry none 'bout that. He'll be fine eating. They're better if you get 'em before they toughen up."

Jimmy cried. He couldn't hold it any longer. The rabbit was brown not white and he was dead not alive. Only the fur on his tiny stomach was gray, Jimmy rolled over and smothered his face onto the pressed grass. His body shook with sobs, but he knew it wasn't an excuse.

"What's wrong, Jimmy?" Larry asked. "Christ sakes, what's eat'n' ya?"

"Nothing. My shoulder hurts, that's all. The gun hurt me when I shot it."

"That's nothing," Larry lowered his voice. "Mine hurt for a

whole week on my first kill. 'Course I shot five that day. Father'll be proud of you though."

Jimmy sat up and the gun fell from his lap. He pulled out the red handkerchief and blew his nose violently.

"Do you think he will really be proud of me?"

"Sure. I'm sure of it. You'll make a good hunter. Come here and watch me slice 'em."

More tears came. Jimmy knew the rabbit's stomach had to be cut. His father had told him that the insides had to be torn out, but he cried anyway.

"Still hurt, huh?" Larry asked. "Here, let me rub it."

The tall, lanky youth threw the dead rabbit at Jimmy's feet and leaned over his brother. The strong youthful hands of his brother felt good, but Jimmy continued to stare at the rabbit, dead beneath his feet.

"How's that feel?"

"I feel better." Jimmy stopped crying.

Larry pulled the sharp hunting knife from its sheath, rolled the rabbit onto its back and sunk the blade expertly into the smooth skin. He jerked the knife upward inside the stomach as Jimmy watched with amazement. The skin raised in tent fashion then came apart with a quick thrust of the knife.

"You got to learn how to do this, Jimmy," Larry said digging his bare hand into the open wound. "You got to make sure the rabbit's not sick."

"Yeah, I know, if he's got spots then you can't eat him." Jimmy said pressing his lips flat against cold teeth.

"That's right. See this? It's clean so he's a good kill. Now you tear out his guts and put the rabbit in your coat." Larry tossed the intestines aside.

"He's your rabbit," he said raising the bloody fur toward Jimmy.

"No!" Jimmy shouted. "You carry him. I don't want to get my coat dirty yet."

"Christ sakes, you got to dirty it sooner or later. Here, don't be a kid."

Jimmy opened the coat and Larry dropped the bundle of fur into the deep pocket.

"Larry, I want to go home now," Jimmy said wiping his eyes. "I want to go home and show it to mother...and father."

"Sure thing," Larry answered. "But don't show it to mom. She'll give you the old sermon about killing things. First clean it then she won't make a fuss when it looks like store meat."

"I won't tell mother, but let's go home."

Larry could not hear his brother. He walked toward the shallow creek.

"Larry! Let's go home? I got the kill. Please Larry? Before it's too late?" Jimmy shouted the last words.

"Wait a minute," his brother yelled back as he walked slowly into the thickness of the hollow. "There's plenty of time before dinner. I think I see another rabbit. Load up."

Larry turned and stared at Jimmy, who was still wiping his eyes.

"Now load up and let's just wait a bit." Larry plunged again into the thickness and Jimmy followed.

"No Larry. It's getting late, and it ain't early no more. I got the kill, what else do you want?"

What could he want, Jimmy thought running after his brother. I killed and I liked it. What more does he and father want? The rat was there and I killed it, and the fish was on the end of my line and I jerked its fins off and killed it too, but that's not the same 'cause Larry said it wasn't. But neither was killing the rat 'cause he would have bit me. The rabbit is the same as the fish but it wasn't 'cause it didn't have warm blood so Larry said, but why should I kill the rabbit or the enemy if for no reason?

Then Jimmy remembered how it felt to kill the rabbit, and he began to follow Larry willingly.

"The blood might detract them," Larry said wiping it from Jimmy's jacket. "Let's move on. Wait! The bushes are moving over there!" Larry pointed toward the creek. Jimmy saw the scene again. He felt his shoulders contract, but he did not load his gun. This was Larry's kill.

"They're coming this way!" Larry shouted lifting the 16 gage to his shoulder.

"It looks like two of 'em. No! Maybe three! We'll get 'em all. Quick! Load your gun!"

He did not see that Jimmy leaned the gun against his hip with the stock sinking into the top soil. The young brother looked with admiration toward Larry.

"We'll show 'em who's the best! Yeah, we'll show 'em with buckshot! They'll not run again!" Larry began to laugh softly resting his head on the stock.

"What are they, Larry?" Jimmy asked. "Who are they?"

"The enemy!"

"And you're going to kill 'em ain't you?"

"The rats!" Larry shouted. "We'll kill 'em! Get your gun loaded!"

"But if they're the enemy then they're like us!"

"That's it! That's it! Warm blood like ours! Get your gun loaded!" Larry laughed and his voice resounded through the hollow.

"No Larry. It's getting late and we got to go home! Mother will miss us. It's later and later and pretty soon there'll be darkness and we won't be able to see what we're doing." Jimmy fell on his knees and began to cry again.

"Kill 'em! Kill 'em!" Larry was laughing so hard that Jimmy almost didn't hear the three shots. The laughter continued long after the sound of the gun had faded in the hollow.

Butcher's Boy

———————

Marty Sissors worked at the Grimes Slaughter House. The small concern sent meaty products to large Eastern meat companies. Not depending on Clay Town support, Miss Grimes, owner of the company, paid high wages and was selective in employing her men. Young Marty liked his job; liked the lazy talk of the workers sitting in the sun sipping morning coffee. Marty liked to feed the large steers.

Daylight broke, shining off the long broad backs of the cattle, and Marty, feeling the warm scent of living beef, leaned against the splintery fence, watching the steers roam about the enclosure. He watched them move slowly. Something inside him motivated envy for the laboring animals, something far away and deep, mysterious, almost occult; something unfathomed, soft and almost rubbery, which he could not explain because he did not know it existed, deep inside, but he watched them move and some god swirled within.

"Har, Marty, cows hungry, har?" Marty turned. Dag Mercer, carrying a large manila envelope, stepped out of an Eastern sun. Dag ran the envelope for Miss Grimes each morning from the warehouse into town. Marty knew she could have had one of the drivers pick up the envelope, but instead, she preferred to give a dollar per week to Dag for the service. Each morning Dag, carrying the envelope tightly, was there when Marty fed the cattle, and the two boys, loving the same thing but not understanding nor caring to understand why they came into an early morning communion, stood against each other's shadow and watched the fat cattle eat.

"Dag, they're not cows."

"Not cows, Marty, I know not cows. They look like cows?" Dag Mercer smiled. Marty Sissors was good. Dag liked his friend, for Marty liked the cows and was good to them.

"They're cattle. Steers!"

"What'd they do if Mousie get loose, har?"

"Better not let that hamster loose here."

"See cows, Mousie! Big, black cows! Hurt you!"

Dag had placed Mousie in his cupped hands and was showing her the large animals.

"They won't hurt her unless she scares 'em."

"I no let her go, Marty, Where cows go?"

"Go?" Marty answered, "They just walk 'round the yard 'less they're on a farm, then they walk in fields."

"Where they go after?" Dag persisted, "Where they go inside?"

Then Marty knew, but he did not know how to explain the butchering ritual. "They're killed, Dag."

"Har, they cut up?" Dag was sad watching sun streaming off the straight backs.

"They're slaughtered and then cut up," Marty continued not wanting to talk about death.

"Why you feed 'em?"

"'Cause I'm paid." Marty was not angry with Dag for not knowing, but he answered abruptly.

"Why they feed cows that die inside?"

"They want 'em fat for the butcher." Marty wished Dag would leave. Instead of feeding the cattle, Marty stroked Mousie's soft fur.

The two youths stared again at the fenced animals. Presently

Marty lifted the feed bucket, walked into the breathing mass and dumped the contents. He did not return to Dag, but rather, pretended work on the far side. Dag gently slipped Mousie into his pocket and walked away waving to his friend. Marty returned the wave and spoke some unheard remark. He could not justify death to someone who felt as he felt. Marty went about his daily routines, chores usually gratifying to him, but this Friday, he was unhappy. It was in the air; the lumbering cattle told him, but he could not understand the presence of death.

Marty Sissors lived with and supported his mother. Mrs. Sissors worked, but her efforts brought little income to the Sissors' family. This job, a job Miss Grimes invented for the son of her best butcher who had died last year, was welcomed to Marty's mother even though she secretly did not want Marty to become a butcher like his father. Each day Marty ran to school after the early morning chores, returned at three fifteen to clean the yards, and at the end of each week, he gave his mother the yellow envelope containing thirty dollars, sweets of labor. Marty had outgrown his first work clothes and now there were rumors voiced from inside that he was to become a butcher apprentice. Shrill, screaming squeals of pigs sounded near the small fenced stock yard. Marty wanted to cover his ears. He started for the inside of the plant, and yet he could not enter. Something held him away from the blood smeared room where his father had once shouted commands. Billy Grazio poked his head around the door and called to Marty. "Want'a you in office!"

Marty advanced knowing he knew before he knew; not wanting to know but advancing against the will. The semi-darkness made Marty's pupils dilate and he smelled death. He smelled life also — sweating men, chewing tobacco, stiff, old working clothes — and he was sick. The squeals pierced and shattered around the room. The boy, coming from crisp freshness of morning, stopped and stared, first with disgust then with fear and finally with hypnotic amazement. He wanted to bolt, but the scene held him. Pigs, caught by hooks attached by chains, moved upward, swung, swaying, along a platform high above Marty's eyes. They bounced on the heavy chains. Marty watched the man in an apron, carrying the sharp round knife. Marty watched as the man jabbed the long point into the pig's neck, and then, high above Marty, the dark red blood streamed far out into a gutter running along the sacrificial platform.

Marty started, stopped, then hurried through the plant toward the offices up front. It was nearing eight o'clock, and he wanted to be released from morning obligations, horrid obligations,

"Marty, you've been here for almost two years. Don't you think it about time to move up?"

"I'm satisfied with my job, Miss Grimes."

"Oh, come, Marty, that job was temporary...until you became adjusted to the plant."

The woman behind the steel desk had a new hairdo with a black tint to cover the graying hair, and Marty wondered why, an owner, an important person like her, would come this early to the plant to hear pigs squealing.

"I think it's a swell job, Miss Grimes. Really I do! I really appreciate it, and mom..."

"But now it's time to move up, Marty." The woman wearing the dark green dress leaned forward.

"We have decided to try you in the pen."

Marty wondered who she meant by we, knowing she owned and operated her father's plant. Even more, he wondered at and feared the new job.

"What's the pen?"

"You don't know? Haven't you been inside at all in the two years?"

"I stay mostly with the cattle, Miss Grimes."

Then the thin woman was pressing a button and not speaking to Marty. Her voice was fast and filled with masculine overtones. The friendly chat had ended. "Bill, come in here!"

No sooner had she released the button and smiled at Marty then Billy Grazio was standing at the glass door. "Bill, take Marty and show him the pen. He'll be working there."

She said no more until Marty began to close the door behind him. "You'll be as good as your father."

Then he shut the door quietly and followed Billy, fearing his new job.

"That's it, kid."

"But it's only a cattle bin."

The squeal came from behind him, and Marty knew he must work in   the sacrificial room, away from the sun on the backs of the cattle. "What must I do here?"

"Kill'a cattle," came the Italian assimilation.

"Kill?"

Billy nodded, studying the boy's movements. Marty fought his emotion inside and kept it to himself.

"How?"

"Club. Gun sometimes. You uz'a twenty-two." Billy pointed to the gun leaning against the wall then smiled.

"It pay'a five dollar more. Miss Grimes, she no forget Max. Your old man, he good worker."

"My father, yes."

Marty withdrew, holding his hand to his cheek as if physically preventing the emotion from escaping.

"He liked to kill, didn't he? He enjoyed this?" Marty asked.

Billy stared over Marty's head as if not hearing the question.

Marty ran, releasing emotion through moving legs. Billy, the foreman, stood amazed, calling to the running youth. "You come work early tomorrow! I show you how! You be good lik'a Max!"

Marty ran along the path leading over the hill and a short

cut to town, always advancing upward, but when he reached the top, Marty fell into a heap and cried. He did not move for some moments, tears staining and chaffing his eyes. His father would have been proud of his son's advancement; however, that was not what made Marty stiffen and begin to descend the path. It was the smile the new job would bring to his mother's lips, and the small comforting breath she would breathe. Then Marty walked the narrow path leading to Clay Town, away from the sun of the hill...

Orderly Sleep

"It should be snowing outside." Abe Tatter spit onto the new floor. "It's cold 'nuff! It's winter, ain't it! There's no reason under heaven why it shouldn't snow, and still it rains!" He spoke to no one except perhaps his inner self.

Abe looked through the window at the rain bouncing off the pavement. It rained and Abe Tatter, awake with the first breaths of morning, let himself sink deep into the leather chair facing the television he was not watching. Heat came and brushed his face. Day was awake outside.

"Heathen!" he shouted at no one, turning off the television. "I don't believe, I can't believe in nothing." It took only one week of retirement until reality came crashing through. Last Friday he was happy with work. He arose, made the fire, ate breakfast, and set out for the plant. Now, without the plant, without work, his thoughts dulled. He sat and stared into the empty set. They just can't buy me off like that, he thought. But Abe knew he had been retired. All week he had dreamed that the lull was only a temporary layoff, but he knew beneath the dream, now, in the warm house with rain outside and reality crashing through the dreary Friday storm — he knew and was unhappy.

Martha entered the room and met the stillness with a smile.

"Sure 'nuff, Abe Tatter, you miss me before I'm gone."

Abe looked up and noticed Martha was dressed to leave. "Mrs. Pin's picking you up?"

"Sure indeed. Now Abe, you're sure I'm not leaving you when you need me? It'll be just a day and you could come along. It'd do you the best good possible."

"The revival would pain me, Martha. I've lost God and I'm a heathen."

The words were simple, the thoughts deep. "Heaven forbid!" Martha smiled and looked through the window.

"The only thing you lost was a job and you're only my unhappy Abe, not a heathen. You just git down in the basement and finish that fine chair you started for the church." She hugged Abe while watching the rain. "Your Martha'll only be gone this horrible Friday day. It's not like Columbus was a million miles away. I've looked so much toward this revival."

"Your old Abe'll be all right, Martha," Abe patted her hand. "Don't you worry. It's just that I'm not used to this quiet and haven't I told you, I've needed this rest."

The affirmation soothed Martha. She walked to the window and adjusted her plants. "My goodness, Abe," she turned. "It's not like you haven't earned retirement, and now you can do all the preaching and readin' you want."

Abe did not answer. He was thinking — for an entire week he had thought. Now he again made that silent decision.

"Without God, how can I preach, how can I be alive!"

"You have God, Abe, you silly man. How could you lose God in just a week?"

"I didn't say I lost Him. How can you lose something which was never there?"

"Shame on you, Abe Tatter. You must not blaspheme like that or you'll be punished."

Abe did not tell her about his required punishment.

"You pray hard while I'm gone, Abe. Hear? You pray and you'll be better. You're just unhappy because they retired you.

And Abe, do pick up the things at the grocery. You poor man, I'm leaving you without a parcel of food."

Abe wanted to tell his wife a thousand stories at once. He felt that if he began one, the rest would automatically jump out, cutting, slicing, their way into the room — all from him, all seeping from deep inside the fissure which now lay exposed, but Abe did not speak, he could not speak, and the stories did not come. Martha was out the door and into Mrs. Pin's car before Abe called out, but the jumble of stories that needed expression became stuck. He only cursed with confusion. He felt the womanly perfume of Martha about the room and smelled the damp new wood.

His decision made. Abe climbed out of the deep leather chair and walked toward the rear of the house. He entered the disorderly kitchen and began setting items in place — all the time hating something in Martha which he loved — finally sweeping the floor then gazing with satisfaction at his work. He busied himself with the other five rooms, straightening, cleaning the disheveled relics of his wife. After the cleaning and ordering was finished he returned to the kitchen and sat at the solid oak table, worn smooth.

Abe circled the date. February twenty-second. It gleaned bright red on the McBridy Funeral Home calendar. The dark lead of the pencil blackened the date, covering other circles traced in blue ink. Satisfied with the circle, now meaning something different than participation in a revival, Abe pushed the calendar to the middle of the table, rose and walked to the built-in oak cupboards protruding above the porcelain sink. Muddy coffee erupted into a glass knob of the pot as he poured a cup full. On his return to the table, he opened the refrigerator door and seized, with quivering fingers, a quarter-filled carton of milk. He stared with satisfaction at the empty shelves, closed the door, and returned to the table. He poured the milk into the cup, adding two teaspoons of sugar, which emptied the round bowl. Now there's nothing left, he thought. Nothing left but this cup full, and he sipped the hot liquid from the chalice allowing air and coffee to mix. His wide forehead wrinkled, and the shallow trenches furrowed until they became thin gray hair. Abe hated cream and sugar in his coffee, but Martha had always used it. He glanced over his shoulder at the bubbling coffee pot that leaked from the narrow spout. Only an hour ago he could not have seen his disfigured reflection in its unpolished metal. Martha's lack of attention had caused rust to accumulate around the edges and black stains covered the luster. He had wanted to buy her a newer coffee pot three years ago, but she would have none of it.

"This'll do 'till God provides us with more money. I won't give it up."

For Abe, the coffee pot represented her complete indifference toward anything new, except the house. He remembered telling her the house looked like a modern reception room housing museum relics. She had laughed and replied, "It's livable."

But the paradox of a modern home just recently furnished, moved into by them, believing in older ways, following past traditions, confused Abe Tatter. Then he did not have time to think through such puzzles. Work had occupied his mind.

Nothing had been discarded in moving from their old, comfortable home. The new wide clothes closets were packed with unmatched gloves, moth-eaten rugs, neatly folded blankets, unusable trinkets, sealed boxes, and a Navy officer's uniforms belonging to a son who would never again need them. But now they had been donated to a rummage sale and would make their ways into useful items for others.

Abe had made an itemized account where all the stored things should be sent, and he did not forget to give his Sunday coat to J.C. Pulton, his enemy. Abe pulled the calendar to him and glanced at the date again as though it may have been outdated, but the numbers on the top corners assured him that it was a new one. His eyelids became heavy, not from lack of sleep, Abe thought, but from the loneliness and inactivity of retirement; not that it had rested him, but the knowledge that it would continue. There had been God until there was no longer God, and there had been work until last week.

"It was bad luck to move," Abe laughed. Asking the question aloud, he answered it silently, thinking that God had stayed with the old house. Then, he thought about the books he had read. Had they turned his love, or was it the world around him, the gray, scientific world? He called them heathens being a heathen himself. They would feel sorry for him, but Abe did not envy them their success gained in a world of split-level houses and steel machines. He missed the smell of horses and he missed his boyhood watching the Blacksmith. Funny he thought about that now. Abe drank the remaining coffee, rinsed the cup in the sink, emptied the coffee pot, and threw the milk carton in the trash can.

The bedroom was shaded in darkness as slivers of light penetrated between corners of closed blinds. Abe sat on the bed and reflected while staring at the picture resting on the dresser.

Friday, no fuckdarnworgodamdaing. Ho, no, pisfucworkie, god godgodgodgod slithateseanbastateing wifcrochsmel. Roses and bonbons. No anniversary dinner this year.

He pulled the last cigarette from a pack and lighted it while sitting on the edge of the bed. His violet Christmas robe seemed black, reflecting in the full length mirror on the closet door. He did not recognize the clean shaven face staring at him from the glass interior. The ears were too large to be his, the nose was too flat, the eyes were black and sinister looking, and the partially balding head belonged to a stranger, distant from the once child-man. He slid from the bed and closed the door, hiding the mirror from view. Sitting on the bed again, Abe rested his chin in his palms, calloused from pushing the rod at the sewer pipe plant. Everything finished. Everything in order. Dideadrisevapoflust he thought. Furniture and clothes sold or will be picked up, godgoodfucherstate, debts paid, car sold, enough in the bank for my god scrufucwordin, the letter he thought, walking across the room and lifting the long white envelope. Abe sealed the letter while walking down the stairs into the living room and slid it beneath the door. Turning, he glanced around the room, passed into the kitchen, and descended the stairs leading to the basement. Only square blotches of dust traced where boxes had lined the walls. Only the half finished chair for the church remained. Satisfied with the emptiness of the basement, he walked back through the kitchen, ascended the stairs and entered the bathroom. The cigarette burned close to his fingers. He snuffed it in the ash tray and then emptied the ash tray into the waste basket. He opened the bottle of pills and twisted the cold water faucet and began taking them. He gagged three times before the bottle was empty. He picked up a hairpin wedged between the bathtub and the wall dropping it quickly into the wastebasket. Returning to the bedroom, he crawled onto the bed propping his head on a pillow and stared at the picture atop the bureau. The woman's face became faint and cloudy. He felt the sudden limpness enter each joint of his long, thin body, and his thoughts became dull, incoherent dreams. The sleep was coming and he was pleased that everything had been put in order. It was his nature. But he regretted this way. It was unmanly, but Abe was a coward. It should have been a gun or a rope — not this feminine way. Everything had to be finished before he could sleep. He would have cheated himself if it had not been set straight, but now he could sleep. Now disorder disappeared, marzfucfailingim. Life was the work of a game.

Martha knew life was the game of work, still, she was praying her way to Columbus, but there was no work in modern houses. You empty your bowels with the push of a button and death comes in colorful cardboard boxes, holding in your God against the rot of progress. The ground grave will be cold, dark, and peaceful.

In the stillness of the house he heard the beating of his heart and the creaking of the new walls straining to settle. He shut his eyes and waited. Dream dead dunes and slip the hand in the hole grabbing the womb until you stretch it wide enough for you, death and sleep to enter, curl between legs of peace and work no more sliver up the legs and feel no pain. No blood hard cudgels to bear the birth of pain only intoxicating smells of the womb to fade onto and sleep away. No life to kink the back only mushrooming stillness and lavender toadstools of beetle dung and smells of snoring calm.

Peacelastcomesleepdreamletloosefearsfallsplatter grow womb.

It was soft at first then louder until Abe Tatter regained semi-consciousness.

"Har! Mr. Tatt! Come after? chair for church. Har! Mr. Abe!" Dag shouted from below. "Got blizzard come down!"

Dag's knocking became louder. The voice would not stop beyond the room. "Har Mr. Tatt! Chair! Chair!"

Oh my god did I lock the door? Abe Tatter asked himself. Ruin everything! He made an effort to rise but some sleep-strength pinned him to the bed. Then he heard the twisting of the kitchen door knob downstairs and felt the sleep of peace...

Good Woman Breakers

"Isn't she made up well. Such a natural smile, as though she were living."

"Thank you, Mrs. Stag," Edna Breakers bowed her head. "Grandma lived a good life."

"Yes siree she did." Mr. Stag peeped over the fur-lined shoulder of his wife. "We had some good times with 'er. Many's the night Mary beat us at bridge." He peeped again at the still body in the casket. "She was a wonderful person."

"More than that. She was a saint." Mrs. Stag sobbed, wiping her tears. The lace handkerchief was unsoiled. "Bringing up wonderful children like Gumpy, Eugene and Agatha. And then taking care of you when your father was sent...there."

"Thank you." Edna unconsciously stroked the pleats of the black skirt. She felt the tight nylons hug her legs. She had not been allowed to wear nylons until she entered her senior year and began working part time at the bank. Edna stood in front of the casket and remembered her grandmother's solemn words, "You'll not wear that stuff as long as I'm around." Edna thought how Larry McBridy hardly looked at her that night at the Youth Center because she was the only girl who had worn bobby-socks and braided hair.

"It's just a shame we didn't see her more these last years," Mrs. Stag continued. "How we all drift apart."

The woman unfolded another crease of her handkerchief. Mr.

Stag took his wife's elbow and led her to a folding chair. McBridy Funeral Home was painted in Gallic print across the seat.

Edna Breakers watched as the couple talked to people. Mrs. Stag was laughing now, not aloud so as to be distinguished above the voices of others, but Edna saw her yellow teeth beneath the pressed lips. Edna turned and walked toward the main door where her older brother and her mother stood talking to Mr. and Mrs. Spears. Edna hated the high school principal. They did not see her approach, Edna, hands on hips, stood motionless on the outer circle listening to the conversation.

"It was so good of you to come."

"Why Agatha, you know how we felt about your dear mother," Mrs. Spears spoke. "George and I have always admired how she put you and Eugene through school…"

"She was so proud of Edna," Mr. Spears broke in. "I remember her crying at Edna's graduation. Though, she had a right to, Edna, valedictorian! She sure was proud of her children…"

"Edna did have help," the tall straight woman who called herself Edna's mother answered playing with a chain attached to her bifocals. The gray hair was perched in a bun behind her head and the shallow wrinkles of her forehead contrasted with the smoothness of the hair. Her long hemline, her wasted body with bones edging forward at the joints, and her black stockings added twenty years to Agatha Breakers' middle age. She had corrected Edna three times for calling her grandma.

"Oh my gracious, Agatha," Mrs. Spears answered, "You certainly were a help, being a teacher. I'm sure Edna couldn't have gotten along without your help, and you were so good to Mary, staying with her."

"Agatha has been a help to all of us," Agatha's brother mumbled. "I thought she'd leave after me, but thank God she stayed on with momma. I haven't been back for five years, you know. Got to keep the presses rolling!"

"Being the eldest, Eugene, this has, no doubt hit you hard?" Mrs. Spears said. And so soon after Gumpy's heroic death."

"Especially since you couldn't make it for your brother's funeral," Mr. Spears added. "It was such a fine funeral."

"But you were so close to Mary, weren't you?"

"It was a shock, Mrs. Spears, but I feel sorry for sis and Edna. They were so near to Momma. Here's Edna all alone," he said turning. "She always kept to herself, even as a pup."

He threw a short stout arm around Edna's shoulder and pulled the girl into the group.

"Don't she look like an angel?" he asked.

"Doesn't, Eugene," Mr. Spears smiled. "You're the same old Eugene. Your mother worried so about your grammar, and now you run a newspaper."

"Grammar and Latin crap keeps you fuddyheads in business. Kids forget most everything when they get out beneath your golden rules."

"Grammar is important, Eugene," Agatha corrected. Her gaze fell on a large basket of red roses beside the door.

"Just like Momma." he laughed. Eugene had not stopped to clean up before coming to the funeral home. Wrinkles had formed on his gray flannel suit while driving the long distance from Portsmouth. A shadow of a beard covered his face and his eyes remained half-opened from weariness.

"George," he turned toward the principal. "Agatha's the spittin' image of Momma."

"She has been faithful," Mrs. Spears answered. "I remember Mary and Agatha walking into the PTA meetings. Sometimes Gumpy accompanied them. It was certainly a scream to see your mother president and Agatha, a member of the faculty, looking on. Yes, Mary did so much for the community, anything she set her mind for, she got. Why the time she came with Agatha to our yearly teachers' picnic and had a fit about Joe Pango spiking the punch. We never had anymore of that."

"Yep," the principal spoke. "Mary and Julie here were the best of friends, despite their..."

"Come George," Mrs. Spears broke in. "We must pay our respects."

Mr. and Mrs. Spears left the group and walked slowly toward the casket which was buried among roses, chrysanthemums, pansies, and banners bearing the names of relatives and friends. Eugene motioned Agatha and her daughter away from the door. Agatha stood leaning against a hat rack, her wiry smile greeting each new visitor, her head bowing mechanically with each smile. Edna picked a flower from the basket of roses and began rubbing it between her palms. The petals fell to the floor in rolled balls.

"Edna! Stop that! That's childish. It's disrespectful." Agatha raised her almost masculine like voice. "People will talk! You and your casual insincerity. I'm going to give you a good talking to after this. Mother and Gumpy were too easy with you. You'll mind with me!"

"When will it be over?" Edna asked stuffing the flower back into the basket. "I'm tired. I don't like all these people, and just before the funeral."

"Now child," Agatha began. "It's a tradition. These are your mother's friends. You must behave like a lady for once."

"You poor kid," Eugene broke in. "I bet you're beat. You've been at this for the past two days. Why don't you go out an' sit on the porch?"

"Eugene!" Agatha snapped! "The funeral will start in fifteen minutes and Edna must begin to discipline herself. She doesn't have mother and Gumpy around any more to take her part." Eugene examined his wrist watch.

"'Tis so peaceful she is," a stooped woman, who had returned from the casket, stood before them. She extended a shaking hand to Agatha, who grasped the shriveled bones in both hands. The woman's eyes were hidden deep in her head; her glasses rested on a stump of a nose that had shrunken, leaving folds of skin to bounce as she talked. Her voice blended an Irish brogue through cracked lips. It glided softly into the buzz of the room,

"Holy Mary. 'Tis a hard life she led. 'Tis so indeed. 'Twon't be the same. 'Tis a shame, 'tis indeed. She 'twas a good woman. Angel food cakes 'twas her only fault."

"Mrs. Flutters," Agatha spoke with a slight quiver entering her voice, "you know Edna, my daughter, and this is the oldest of the family, brother Eugene."

"Why of course I know Kathleen Flutters," Eugene interrupted.

"I should know her. I cut her grass when I was no higher than a lump of sugar."

"'Twas Mary herself who said you'd become rich," Mrs. Flutters answered shaking his hand. "'Twas she said ye went to Portsmouth. 'Twas she showed me the betrothal a bit back. 'Twas the lass of a newspaper man she said you'd married. 'Twas so, indeed, a handsome lass, bit plump but 'tis a sign of health."

"Mrs. Flutters's sharp," Eugene laughed nervously. "Me Kate," he said imitating her Irish accent. "For kickin' eighty you'd be a wit. Me good mother wrote me about ye..." He fell again to mumbling. "About your angel food cakes, I mean."

"Agatha, me darlin," she turned toward the school teacher. "'Twas a glorious deed Mary did when I fell and broke me leg. 'Twas she looked over me."

Mrs. Flutters leaned close to Agatha and whispered. "'Twas I that sent over the food for ye. 'Twas an angel food cake and ham roast for the family."

"Thank you so very much, Mrs. Flutters. But you shouldn't have."

"'Tis God's shame that Jude and Gumpy 're not here. 'Twas

a good man he, and Gumpy too, if only Jude'd not have left blessed Mary and joined the war. 'Twas mercy's shame, leaving her to tend a month old lass. 'Twas not his fault he'd never return, God's mercy upon them both."

"Dad was an adventurer," Eugene spoke. "I'm his spitting image, they tell me."

"'Tis a crying day if ye go to war," Mrs. Flutters answered. "'Twill be your wife to bury."

"Don't worry about that, I'm four-F," Eugene opened his wrinkled suit coat and gripped his belt with two over-stuffed hands.

"Yes, Eugene has a sickness," Agatha answered.

"It has to do with his rectum," Edna broke in watching the line of people gather around the casket. She wondered why each person had to read the white cards attached to the flowers.

"That's most inappropriate, Edna," Agatha answered.

"'Tis the crosses we carry for God's mercy," the Irish woman looked into Eugene's eyes. He did not return her quizzical glance. Rather, his gaze had met the eyes of a middle age blond entering the room through the back door. His line of vision was half-way up the tall frame when Mrs. Flutters again spoke.

"Jude 'twas a fine man, but 'tis a shame they'd not let his soul rest in peace, sayin' he'd run from Mary. She loved him truly, God's mercy upon us, 'twas all she'd talk, till now."

The woman turned toward the casket and bowed her head. "'Tis God's wonder why'd a man 'twould want to leave an angel? And your man, me darlin'!" Mrs. Flutters spoke to Agatha. "Carted away to that horrible place. 'Twas a good mind he had, though they'd say 'twas not."

"We don't talk about him," Agatha answered quickly.

"Let me find you a chair," Eugene suggested. She followed him along the path separating the chairs until he guided her into the fifth row.

Edna turned suddenly toward her mother. "Was Granddaddy really as bad as everyone says?"

"He was mean. He left mother without a dime when the First World War broke out. He may have been killed in action, winning some stupid medal, but it left mother a broken woman. She did everything in her power to raise us."

"You and Eugene and Gumpy worked," Edna said, "and I helped."

"She never allowed you to dirty your hands. No, indeed, we always waited until you went to bed and redid the dishes. Mother wouldn't hurt your feelings by telling you that you didn't know how to do them. She spoiled you rotten. You always got to watch your programs on television. You always had it easy. You and that no good Eugene! She spoiled you both rotten. And he up and left us, not a penny, mind you. Just left us for that wealthy whore in Portsmouth."

"I gave her all I made at the bank this year." Edna picked another rose from the basket.

"Mother didn't have a fault in the world," Agatha answered as though she had not heard her daughter. "Maybe she was a little hard with us, especially me, I was never allowed the freedom you enjoyed. I always had to be in by nine o'clock when I was growing up, but she meant well. She knew that crazy father of yours too. You take after him, but mother always treated you like her child. You should be thankful that she talked me into keeping my maiden name. You'd still have his name if it hadn't been for mother. She picked up after you and made sure you didn't get into trouble with men, like I did with him."

"Will the funeral last long?"

"You'll never understand," Agatha shook her head. "Wait until you get a man. Yes, it's going to be a long funeral. Just wait till you get one of those clawing beasts."

"Everyone is here. There's Jo and Irene Pango, I must say hello."

Agatha left Edna alone. The girl patted her new hairdo watching older, bent people shake their gray heads over the coffin and shuffle to the wooden chairs. Suddenly a familiar voice called to her from the doorway.

"Hey Edna. It's me, Nancy."

"Come on in. Gee, thanks for coming. I'm bored to death."

"Sorry to hear 'bout your grandmother, I would've dropped down last night but I had a date with John. All the kids at the bank send regrets. Have any of 'em dropped in?"

"Haven't seen any," Edna answered shifting her feet as though keeping time with music. "I tell you, Nancy, I'm going spastic. All these good-doers really give me nerves!"

"I know what you mean. But honestly, Edna, aren't you just crushed with your grandmother passing away so quick? She really helped you out."

"Sure. I'm going to miss her," Edna answered. "But she was so goddamn strict. Everybody's making over her, but half these straights hated her. She was always giving them hell."

"You're kidding?"

"See George and Helen Spears over there? Mrs. Spears hated Grandma 'cause Grandma got to be Treasure then President of the PTA. Grandma really was way out of bounds taking the job. She only wanted it to spite Mrs. Spears. I heard her tell mom that Mrs. Spears was no better than her and that she could be President as good as anybody else. And there's Bill Bord and his wife. Grandma use to give him holy hell for puttin' our milk on the front porch. She wanted him to knock at the door and deliver it, and him with the whole town to deliver to. It was always like that. She picked at people, especially mom. I think that's why dad went out of his tree. There's Fanny Stag and Clarence. They sat there all day yesterday. I don't know why she's crying.

Fanny and Grandma fell out a long time ago. Grandma slammed the door in her face one time when Fanny said Eugene would be nothing but a drunk and a bum. That's before he skipped to Portsmouth. They really had it then. Grandma never allowed Fanny's dog in our back yard. 'Bout the only person here who's sorry is poor Mrs. Flutters, and she's too old to know better.

I guess she's scared 'cause she's got to die soon."

"Hey, did you hear that Frank Messer got beat up at the Westway last night?" Nancy asked playing with an empty coat hanger on the rack behind her.

"Good for him," Edna replied. "I wish I could have been there. You know, I never was in the Westway. Christ, I'm never allowed to go anywhere."

Edna led Nancy across the room. They sat in the last row of chairs and continued to talk, their hands gesturing with each syllable.

The swaying bottom of Eugene Breakers left Mrs. Flutters. She had started a monologue with Mr. and Mrs. Yanks. He retraced short steps across the room toward Marcia Dur. The beautician had dyed her hair since he saw her last, five years ago, but her long, shapely legs and heavy breasts had not changed since that farewell meeting in his car.

"Marcia Dur," he whispered. Long blond curls swept across her shoulder as she turned. She looked at him for a moment without speaking. "By Christ, Gene, you got fat," she said breaking the stare.

"That's the newspaper world," he replied. "Plenty of support for old age. I see you got the same shape."

"Your mother looks so peaceful."

"We'll all miss her," he answered taking Marcia's arm and leading her toward the door. "She was a perfect dear."

"How's your wife?"

"She stayed in Portsmouth. Got to have someone watching over things, ya know."

"Have any children yet?"

"Hell no. Don't wish that on a happy adventurer."

"Are you happy?" He had not released her arm. Marcia made no effort to pull away.

"I could be more so."

"Do you miss Clay Town?" She sat in a chair against the wall, but he continued to hold her arm.

"I miss what's in it. You know, this terrible shock and all. I wish I had a drink. Maybe we could scoot out to my car and have a fast one. I sure need it."

"I'm taken," she answered walking beside him.

"Where's the body? And who in hell is it?"

"Catty Willomenia. He's up in Columbus at some queer school learnin' 'bout make-up. Say's he's gonna take me to Hollywood, but it'll be a bitch of a day when I leave here. Maybe I will though."

"You lonely?"

"I could be more so. I'm not. There are ways."

"My car's too beat up to be in the funeral. They're furnishing those big black ones, ya know. Want to join me at my private bar in the alley?"

"You still hittin' that stuff?"

"You have anything better?"

"Try sniffing glue."

They left the smell of flowers. Eugene did not release her elbow as they walked behind the funeral home. He opened the door of the old Ford and Marcia ducked quickly into the front seat. She stared ahead as the shadows of the alley played with the dash board.

"We only got five minutes," he said reaching beneath the seat and pulling a bottle of scotch onto his lap.

"Beat up car but good scotch. Gene, you're still crazy."

"This is my spare car, I let the wife keep the new Chrysler, prestige around town, ya know."

"Yeah, I know. Are you really an editor?"

"Naw, I wouldn't handle a pencil, I'm manager of the whole works."

"You sure jumped up fast. When you left here you had nothing,"

Marcia smiled.

"That's the breaks and having a rich wife."

"Yeah, I know," Marcia answered crossing her legs, smoothing her black satin dress and taking the open bottle which he offered.

"Here's to Mr. Big!" She swallowed a mouthful, made a face, and breathed deeply. He took the bottle from her and tilted it against his lips.

Eugene rested his right hand on her knee. His two diamond rings glittered in the mirror of the compact which she had taken out to inspect her hair.

"It's a shame," she said staring into the shadows. "Your mother's lying in there dead and you're out here boozing it up with a married woman."

"A little drink ain't gonna hurt nobody. It helps me meet the sorrow, besides, Momma didn't do much for me. We fought most of the time till she drove me out'ta the house. I just couldn't stand her no more. She tried to be good, but Christ, she made us miserable. If it wasn't for her, I would've stayed here and married you." He turned toward Marcia and she understood his eyes even though shadows had crept across his face.

In the viewing room, a nervous Agatha approached Edna and Nancy. "Where's Eugene? I've been looking all over for him?"

"I don't know. He was with Mrs. Flutters last time I saw him."

"There he is, with Marcia Dur," Nancy pointed. "Over there, coming in the door."

Agatha turned her head sharply when Nancy mentioned Marcia Dur.

"I bet he's been outside with that trash!" Agatha said, breathing deeply. "I'll break this up in a hurry!" She scurried between the chairs toward her brother.

"Man! Is Marcia Dur a wild one!" Nancy said. "She's got every man in town chasing her, including your brother. She did the Moon-dog in the Westway last week and the bartender had to stop her."

"I envy 'er," Edna said. "I'm going to get out of this town so I can live it up. Everyone knows you here and they tell your parents if you spit on the street. Now, nothing's going to stop me!"

"You're going to quit the bank?"

"When I save up enough money. I'm going to live when I leave this hole."

"What will your mother say? She's not going to let you go."

"Mom's headed for the nut house. She's tried to kill herself twice now. Only Grandma stopped her. Mom's going to end up like dad, but I'm not going to wet nurse her."

"Did she really try to kill herself?"

"My deepest sympathy is with you, Edna," the Reverend Seward said poised gracefully across two vacant chairs in order to whisper the message. The two girls stood immediately.

"Thank you Reverend. I'm so glad you're going to give the sermon.

Grandma and Gumpy liked your sermons so much."

"Thank you child. I hope I may comfort those remaining. It

was such a shock to the congregation. Most of them are here to bid her farewell. She was such a wonderful woman."

"Thank you Reverend."

"I think perhaps you'd better go sit in the front row with your mother and Eugene. I'm about to begin the service. It's good that youth can console youth, but now you must gather with your own, Edna!"

Edna followed Reverend Seward to the front row of chairs. He greeted Agatha and Eugene.

"This is all of the surviving family?" he asked the gray-haired school mistress.

"Yes Reverend, we are all mother had in the world, but she had so many close friends."

"May I start the service now?"

"Yes, by all means,"

He walked to the stand beside the casket. It had held the guest book, but the minister placed a Bible and a page of notes on the empty top. He poised both hands as though being robbed. The noise of the room subsided until only a few isolated sobs broke the stillness.

"Dear friends, we are gathered here today," he began. Edna's thoughts tried to concentrate, but they ended in confusion. She told herself that it was proper to think only about her Grandmother, but city lights, honking horns, clicking glasses, and the smell of crowded streets continued to enter unseen into the flower scented room and dazzled her sorrow into a corner from which it darted only once when the minister's voice raised and pronounced in slow distinct syllables.

"She was a good woman."

Eugene sat beside Edna gently patting her arm and staring toward the back of the room where Marcia's dress was raised high. He could accomplish this unnoticed since the family chairs were arranged in a semi-circle. Marcia sat in the back of the room, but her legs reached lusciously into the aisle. Eugene wondered if she was bothering Reverend Seward. Agatha moved nervously about in her chair. She bit her fingernails, and once slapped Eugene's arm when she spied him picking his nose."

"So friends, let us bow our heads in memory of one who is resting in His House, for she raised three responsible children who have prospered in the community. Yes, with all her hardships, she was a worthy and gracious member of the church and a sister to all."

Reverend Seward ended his talk and a prolonged silence overcame the room for the first time. Eugene led Agatha to review the casket. Edna followed. A procession of shifting feet moved slowly behind the family. Slowly, slowly they materialized outside the large brick funeral home and walked toward the waiting cars. Each car carried a small flag attached to the window announcing a funeral was in progress. The family was swallowed into the leading car.

Mrs. Flutters broke into a run and overtook the black Chrysler before the door closed. She leaned inside and spoke in tearful sobs.

"'Twas a good woman. Bless her soul! Ye children should thank the grace of God for His Blessing. 'Twas a good mother she. God bless ye all. 'Twas a good woman."

The ancient figure shuffled quickly down the street and turned a corner. She was nowhere in sight when the car left the curb. It followed behind the thick tires of the hearse, and the black clothed casket could be seen through the rear window...

The Move

Paul Steiner and his mother climbed the steep cement steps maneuvering carefully over the large cracks. The crevices zigzagged beneath the melting slush. The mansion became larger with each step upward until they reached the top of the hill overlooking the snow-covered parking area below. Mrs. Steiner stopped to rest, expelling deep breaths. Paul pulled the collar of his overcoat tightly against his neck and watched his mother's breath become fog. She nodded her head, supporting a fur-lined turban hat. Paul walked the remaining five steps, stepped onto the small open porch, approaching the oak door, slammed the tarnished brass door knocker against the cracked wood and stood back in anticipation. The door opened and Paul saw a black leather jacket move into the doorway. The jacket moved toward him with the arms and a tiny head appearing suddenly, but the black leather back did not stop. It shuffled toward Paul with swaying, awkward steps until he and his mother were forced to step from the small porch. They watched the mover, as they remained in the drifted snow against the mansion walls.

Paul's eyes swept to the third floor of the dirty gray mansion, but the strawberry colored kite was no longer there. The window pane was broken, discolored yellow curtains hung through sharp edges of glass. The house stood as firm as a gray medieval castle which Paul had seen in a movie. He tried to forget that its height was not there, high on the hill overlooking Clay Town, but he did not forget. On cold damp mornings when he scanned the sky wondering if it would storm, the gray walls reflected the sun streaking through the depressing clouds, or when he laughed, surrounded by a group of friends walking home from Sunday mass, his gaze seemed mechanically to raise and settle on the two turrets pointing into the sky from each extreme of the mansion. Alone, topping the highest hill of Clay Town, the shadow of the Ottoman mansion reminded Paul that there was life higher than his. Johnny Ottoman had shown him this life, high on the hill, after they became friends at Larry McBridy's birthday party. But Paul had never returned to the Ottoman mansion after standing under that early Friday morning rain, seven years past. Paul's mouth became dry when he mentioned Johnny's name, and the funeral, so he did not talk to others about his boyhood friend, but Paul felt the same deep hole gnaw inside him when he thought about the stiff-legged pallbearers carrying the ruby red coffin.

The leather jacket passed in front of Mrs. Steiner and her son. The mover backed out of the door carrying an armchair. Without noticing the onlookers to his left, he labored down the hill to a truck in the snow covered parking lot. Paul followed his mother through the thick oak door frame. She came to a stop in a corner of the family room. Paul was behind her, twisting his delicate hands. He listened to her address the two old women seated in a dark nook of the wide, empty room, shuffling his feet against hardwood floors recently peeled naked by the mover.

Paul felt as if he was standing outside the mansion looking in the window gazing at a surrealistic scene. He peeked over his mother's shoulder at the two women sitting side by side on faded velvet chairs, gazing from the obscurity of shadows. They sat rigid and dainty. Bending slightly forward in the chairs, they smiled and nodded their heads — chickens at roost. Blood scarlet draperies folded behind them making the small wrinkled faces look like blotches of white powder. The draperies and chairs seemed alone in the room. Mrs. Steiner's voice echoed shrill in the emptiness,

"Couldn't come sooner. So much to do in town. This place is so out of the way. Your road is practically impossible to climb in the new model cars they make now-a-days. Snow drifts almost three feet deep in some places, but here we are."

His mother pulled at Paul's coat sleeve to step forward for inspection, but his inner self remained outside. She pointed to the lady on the right and told Paul that Mrs. Clara Ottoman did not remember him as a baby with his long wavy blond hair, but that Miss Mona Ottoman, wearing a crisp starched summer dress in the middle of winter — did remember him. "It was simply amazing," she continued, "that dear, dear Mona had remembered." Mrs. Steiner had volunteered Paul for service. "The phone call did seem urgent, and the Steiners and the Ottomans were such good friends even though the Ottomans were almost all, well, gone. You two are the only ones left after Billy passed away. How long was it since Paul visited Johnny, oh yes, many years."

His mother droned on, apologizing for the absence? "Johnny was a fine boy. He'd have become an important man if he'd have lived. He'd be president of Plant number three. Business wouldn't have lost control if Johnny... Moving south, never heard of such a thing. Just because labor's cheap. But Paul really did feel awful 'bout Johnny's death, that's why he never came up."

Mrs. Steiner's shrill voice did not disturb the absent stare of Clara, who wore a black cotton dress. She looked past Mrs. Steiner and Paul, unconcerned that Clay Town residents were uncovering from a blizzard, or that Paul had come to help take them from the Ottoman mansion into a one story house on the South Side.

Mona, aware of each movement, raised a thin right hand and waved a circle sending Mrs. Steiner scampering across the empty room and into the whiteness outside. Paul stood at attention, mute, stiff, and all the while hoping they would dismiss him from obligations, standing, knowing, they intended to use him since the important telephone call had come at seven-thirty in the morning. Clay Town people, now in winter, were only sipping their first cup of coffee at such an early hour, when the call came from Mona, so the call had become an important topic at once.

"I suppose you want me to help the movers?" Paul asked. "I'd better get started. Mom's going to walk home. It isn't far down."

"I remember you as a youngster," Mona said rubbing an empty ring worn third finger. "You knew Johnathan, before. You and he went fishing together, and Johnathan invited you here every Friday afternoon, that is, until he contracted pneumonia. And here it is, another Friday."

"Yes, but those Fridays happened a long time ago, I'm twenty-two now. I never wanted to come back."

"You loved Johnathan, didn't you?"

"Yes."

"What, who are you speaking about?" Clara asked, rubbing her right knee beneath the cotton dress.

"He's a friend of Johnathan's," Mona had to shout. "He's come to help us, to help you."

"Johnathan's friends are welcome. You know that, Mona. He can stay, but we must be good to him. We don't get many visitors these days."

Mona turned in the velvet chair and whispered, "Poor Clara, she is partially deaf, you know. She's never been the same since. I'm afraid this move will kill her. We are the last of the Ottomans, young man. I suspect you know that. Your father will be glad now. We're all that is left to hurt him."

"Dad has never said anything." It was a convenient lie.

"He should have. He should have young man." Mona trembled in the summer dress, "He should praise us to God. It was our reputation which started him, and he never thanked us."

"I don't know what Dad has done to you," Paul answered, "but he's never spoken badly about you. We respect the Ottomans as everybody does."

Paul turned toward the large bay window facing the hill and pointed to the white covered town below.

"Respect!" Mona laughed. "No one ever respects wealth. They fear it, Paul Steiner. Everyone fears wealth until they can drag it down into their muck, and when they're all playing in it and do not know what to do with their small fortunes, then they don't fear wealth any longer. That's our position now toward the town people. But forgive me. I have a job for you, but first let's tour the home. The last tour of the Ottoman House. I want you to see Clay Town as we have seen it these years, as Johnathan's friend and as a Steiner, you have command of the house for the present. It will presently go, like everything else. They're turning it into a nursing home, you know."

"Yes, I know," Paul answered. "It'll be a nice spot for a nursing home," he said taking off fur-lined gloves and rubbing his chin.

"A real Steiner, you." Mona twitched in the wrinkled face but her eyes glistened, "Yes, Mrs. Leveler has made a good investment."

"We have Johnathan's fishing gear," Clara said suddenly. "Don't we, Mona?"

"No!" Mona shouted then calmed again. "We sold it. Johnathan loved to fish with you." She turned to face Paul.

"Yes, I never fish much anymore," he said.

"Time passes. People pass," Mona replied, "father, mother, Johnathan, Dr. Gilley, Billy, and John Paul Jones. We are the only ones left. Only us and this home. The home passes to others.

We pass to." She made a sweeping motion with her right hand. "And now they're taking it."

Clara was five years younger than her sister, but as she sat rubbing a hidden knee and chewing a piece of gum, her parched, wrinkled face and shriveled body appeared much older.

"It is a beautiful place," Paul forced himself to say.

"It isn't as beautiful as when all the family was here. No home is pretty without a large family even if it has ivory and gold. Come, let me show you what they're going to do to our home."

She extended her hand and Paul helped her rise from the chair. Crouched forward, hunched back and withered, she tilted her head to glance at Paul Steiner.

"You see, young man, the Ottomans have fallen." She turned to her sister. "I shall show Johnathan's friend through our home, Clara."

"What?"

"I'm going to show Johnathan's friend through the house."

"Oh, he can't see Johnathan's toys now. We have the fishing things packed, and the rest has been sold or thrown into the trash."

Mona patted Clara's arm then led Paul into the dining room. He followed until the old woman stopped beneath a chandelier missing half its ornaments.

"I wonder what they'll do with the boatswain lamp?"

"Boatswain lamp?" Paul asked.

"Yes. Billy called it the boatswain lamp. Heaven only knows where he acquired the name. Probably from the war, I suppose. It's a little too big to be called such a lamp."

She tilted her head to study the chandelier. "Don't you think?"

"I don't know what a boatswain lamp is."

"Billy never told us either. He called everything in the house by sea names. My goodness, we chowed down in the mess hall and the reception room was the quarterdeck, and the back porch was the fantail, Billy always wanted to sail. You know, he was in the First World War. Come," she shuffled forward, "let me show you the quarterdeck."

Paul followed Mona through the family room and into the reception parlor where he had entered. Walking onto the quarterdeck, she ordered two men to stop and lower a mahogany bookcase to the hardwood floor before they carried it into winter.

"We had eight of these," she said, "two of them were in Johnathan's room. You know, we kept everything exactly in order. But we cannot take his things with us to the house. We sold seven. This one we're keeping for our silver and crystal. We kept only two sets of silver. We had to sell the others. The ones we have are the best."

Mona continued on in brisk sentences, "Clara's husband, Dr. Gilley, ordered it special. He was such a splendid man, and in no time at all after their wedding, Dr. Gilley became one of the family. Those were the days of youth and gaiety when The Captain, that's what we called father because Billy called him Captain, the Captain and mother held parties, and friends came all the way from New York and Boston and Newport. Then the shock of Johnathan's death following the Captain and mother's fatal accident by only three years unnerved Clara, and she began taking too much medication."

Mona became possessed. She could not stop talking. She was reaching into the grab-bag world of her soul. "Poor man. Clara's grievances affected Dr. Gilley and he soon joined them up there."

She tilted her head and looked at the chandelier hanging in the dining room. "But let me show you sick bay."

She motioned the two men to carry the bookcase outside into winter. She pushed aside the door and led Paul into a vacant library with small windows high up the walls. One piece of furniture remained.

"This is The Captain!" Mona exclaimed pointing toward the portrait hanging on the opposite wall. The picture was hung over an unused fireplace. The broad, solemn face peered at them from the dark canvas. Shallow cracks wrinkled it as though it was a shattered mirror. Paul moved closer. He read aloud the printing on the gold label below the picture, <u>Samson Rodney Ottoman, 1942.</u>

"Yes, it was painted a year before he and mother died," she said. "That's why we asked your mother to bring you over. The Captain is everything to us. We want you to move him and Clara's medicine chest. You're a relative, and by being a relative, you will keep the chest a secret."

"Me? A relative to you?" Paul exclaimed.

"Yes, a third cousin on your father's side. We wouldn't want The Captain to be moved by any stranger. I thought about you this very morning, so I called. It's such a relief."

"Why wasn't I told that I'm a relative to the Ottomans?"

"Your father has never approved of us. He thought us snobs."

"That didn't stop him from telling me?"

"He might have told you if you hadn't taken a liking to Johnathan, but he thought you would become like <u>us</u> if you knew you were of the Ottoman blood. But it doesn't matter now. The Ottomans no longer can hurt him. The Captain won't like it where he's going. There isn't room there they tell me, but we'll make room if I must give up my bed."

She wiped the gold label beneath the picture with her twisted fingers. "Yes, The Captain would be disappointed, but there is so little left. We had to dismiss the maids. Only Filly is staying on, and she is moving into the house with us. Our new house will be on one floor so Clara won't need to climb so much. Filly will live in the attic which Mrs. Leveler has converted into an extra room.

But oh, my goodness, how will all the rugs and tapestries fit? Mrs. Leveler has told me she put our things neatly into the house, but I suspect she has thrown much away. She snoops, you know."

Leaving sick bay and walking onto the sun porch, Paul stared at the stacked furniture worn bare around the edges. Much of the fringe was missing and the upholstery was streaked with yellow spots showing bare threads. The rips revealed the innards. Once deep velvet, the chairs had faded to pink. "Here is where we kept John Paul Jones," she remarked pointing toward a steel bird cage. He went right after Billy died. Our brother loved him so."

"You mean the parrot?"

"John Paul Jones died two years ago. He died quietly in his cage one night a month after Billy passed away. I think John Paul just couldn't live without brother Billy. But our brother had cancer, you know. He merely called it the scurvy, but we knew better. The doctor told us it was cancer. I went up to his room one morning and he was asleep. When I tried to wake him, he just slept on. John Paul Jones died the same way. He must have sensed that Billy would never see him again and he stopped talking the day after we had Billy buried. Imagine, after seventeen years of talking he quit because he must have known that Billy would never hear him. They're going to knock this out." She pointed toward the wall dividing the sun porch from the family room. "They're going to make it one big room for them. We're exchanging houses, you know."

"No, I didn't know that was the agreement. It's an exchange then?"

"Yes, Mrs. Leveler is giving us her house and she's moving into our home. She's a trained nurse who's sold shares in order to buy our home. She's in charge of the investment so rather than buying a new home, she allowed us to move into hers."

Paul followed Mona again into the quarterdeck. "You must

go up stairs and see Johnathan's place. It will be your last glimpse of it."

"No, no," Paul almost screamed. "I'd rather stay down here, thank you."

"Please," Mona answered softly. "I'm not feeling well and I cannot continue the tour."

He began to walk the winding, narrow stairs, remembering the bounding jumps of pleasure following Johnny to the room where the strawberry colored kite hung in the front window. The room had been both a penny arcade and public library for Paul. The two boys passed long Friday afternoons pretending to be grown-ups. The steel slot machine, bolted to a table, was Paul's favorite game since each Friday he won enough money to attend the movie. Paul did not realize until years later that the machine could be rigged. Climbing the stairs, Paul remembered the times after which they had exhausted the choice of games and everything became silent. They sat looking from the window onto Clay Town. After a few minutes of silence, Johnny would nudge him and shout gleefully, "The Cap owns that plant on the hill, and that one over there, beyond the town, and two more behind us! What does your Daddy own?" Then he would laugh, but Paul knew that Johnny's laughter was not meant to ridicule. Johnny was rich and his wealth was a joke between them. Toys meant nothing to Johnny, who shared unselfishly with Paul.

Stopping on the first floor, Paul remembered the Friday Johnny had laughed when he'd torn the green cloth of the pool table by an awkward shot. But Johnny continually reminded Paul that The Cap was the richer of the two fathers and until his Daddy became rich, Paul was, at the same time, his guest and servant.

Paul reached the second floor where the halls smelled of sickness and medicine. He thought while peeping into empty rooms, how his father had ironically become the richer of the two by starting a boat factory and selling outboards to the middle class businessmen. Paul, at last, could not force himself to enter Johnny's empty room on the third floor. No, he thought, he would remember it by the tattered box kite hanging in the window. Turning on the third floor, he descended the stairs.

Mona had returned to the velvet chair. Both women stared absently from their corner as Paul reentered the dining room.

"Did you enjoy your tour?" Mona asked. Clara continued to rub her knee.

"Yes I did."

"Are you ready to carry The Captain and the medicine chest to our new house?" She pointed to a small chest beneath Clara's chair. Paul had not seen it when entering. The small, worm-eaten wooden trunk resembled a fishing tackle box. Paul nodded. Mona leaned forward again in her faded velvet chair and rested her left hand on the box, but suddenly Clara seemed to awaken. She held her sister's arm. Not a word was spoken, but Paul felt uneasy. Both women remained immobile as Clara's withered hand prevented Mona from pulling the chest out onto the floor.

"It's all right, Clara. Johnathan's friend is going to move it to our new house."

Clara did not speak, nor did she loosen the feeble but determined grip.

"It will be safe with him. He's a friend of Johnathan's, you know."

Clara's tiny face lifted to meet Paul's. He looked at the box, at the red slippers, at Clara's left hand caressing her knee, but he purposely avoided looking into her face.

"Take care of my medicine chest, young man," she said between pressed lips. "It's all I have left in the world, and when it's gone, my world ends."

Paul lifted the chest and carried it to his car. Placing it in the trunk, he returned into the empty library finding Mona admiring The Captain.

"And do take care of The Captain," she said wiping the edges of the picture. "He's everything to me."

She helped Paul take the portrait down and carry it to the door, but she would not enter the cold as though she were afraid of the morning air.

"There you are my dear! I've come to help!" A large buxom woman shouted at Mona as Paul passed through the doorway.

"Hi Paul Steiner!" The intruder patted his arm when he returned. "How's your pa? Haven't seen you people much of late. Bet your pa ain't sellin' a whopping many boats this season?" She laughed big.

"No," Paul answered. "He doesn't sell anything during these bad months, but he keeps busy by converting the rough-boxes that the McBridy Funeral Home throws away into cabinets. He's doing pretty well with 'em."

"Your pa sure came up in the world with 'em hanky-danky boats. I 'member when he was only a truck driver at the Ottoman plant. But so have I come up. How you like my new home? She's a beaut h'ain't she? Yep, ya got to have drive to get along now. Why, with the sewer pipe factories folding up, money's hard to the fist. Still have your job at the Golding plant?"

"Yes, for the time being. I'm afraid they're going to fold." Paul looked at Mona and felt ashamed.

"Too bad you couldn't hold your plant tight, Mona," Mrs. Leveler laughed, throwing her coat over the back of Mona's chair. "A little cash ain't a bad thing ta have. 'Course, prestige don't go with 'em no more. Small people owns 'em nowadays."

"Leveler is going to accompany you to our new house." Mona addressed herself to Paul. "She'll show you where to place The Captain."

"H'ain't such a big place." The bosom of the woman shook

when she laughed. "But it's been home to me. But whee, I don't know how I managed to get all this <u>stuff</u> in it? 'Course, it's better this way 'cause they'll be on one floor and won't have to run up stairs all the time to go to the toilet."

An awkward silence fell. Mona's eyes searched the bare wooden floor, Clara mumbled something unheard by the others.

"Would you help Clara onto the sun porch, Mrs. Leveler?" Mona finally asked. "I think she would enjoy the view much better there."

"Sure thing, Dearie," Mrs. Leveler replied taking two quick steps toward the shrunken Clara. She lifted the old woman and carried her from the room.

"I'm afraid she doesn't know how to handle these things. Knocking out walls and throwing two of our good pictures in the trash, and goodness knows how many other things she has destroyed," Mona said pushing Mrs. Leveler's coat onto the floor. She reached down and picked up the coat replacing it on the chair.

"Please don't show Mrs. Leveler the medicine chest. You understand! Send her on some errand. I do hope you've put it in the trunk of your automobile," Paul nodded. "Good," she continued. "Here is the key to our bedroom closet, and when Mrs. Leveler is out slip the chest in there and leave the key under a bed pillow. Goodness only knows, she probably has a duplicate key."

Paul turned and walked toward the door. "You won't need to return here, Paul Steiner. We can manage. Mrs. Leveler and her husband will drive us to the house this afternoon. We'll remember you as Johnathan's friend."

Paul again nodded his head and pulled the leather gloves over his hands.

"Let it be our secret," Mona shouted to him as he started to climb down the cement steps.

Paul started the car, turned on the heater, and waited for Mrs.

Leveler, who ran down the stairs and jumped into the rider's seat as if the cold air would vaporize her.

"They're two nice old ladies," Mrs. Leveler commented wiggling into the seat. "But this was bound to happen to 'em. Just coopin' themselves up in that place. Now there ain't nobody to help 'em."

"Your house is on Royal Street, isn't it?" Paul asked. The snow tires bumped over the graded road sloping down into Clay Town.

"Yeah. I call it a shack now that I got a genuine mansion. Hubby and me have a good time pretending we're the ritzy 'cause we're moving into that place. Just think, Maud Leveler taking over the Ottoman mansion and them moving to my place. It's a riot!" She laughed slapping the dashboard with both hands.

"They let them plants go under 'cause they didn't know how to take care of 'em," she continued. "The old man was the captain of industry, if you know what I mean." She jerked her thumb toward the oil painting resting in the rear seat.

"They're just too lazy to mind business. Besides, Clara couldn't manage a tinker toy 'cause she takes dope."

"Dope?"

"Yeah, the way I hear it, her doctor husband left her 'nuff to supply China."

"I thought they kept to themselves?" Paul asked. "How did you hear?"

"They had maids, didn't they? I guess Clara has been sticking with it ever since, hell, since she lost her old man. They say she keeps the stuff in a little chest. And that Billy was crazy. If you ask me, I think he was a queer. But it ain't none of my business."

Paul looked at the house on the hill, changed now to a silhouette against a dull winter sky. Mrs. Leveler had not eased the guilt feeling inside him. The sewer pipe workers' union had ruined the two old women, and he was an official of the organization.

Swinging the car into a narrow space guarded by a parking meter, Paul dropped a nickel into the machine and followed Mrs. Leveler's long steps into the one story yellow house. He was careful not to lose balance on the warped boards of the porch, fearing he would drop The Captain.

"Hang it over there," she pointed to the wall opposite the front door.

Thick throw rugs were scattered on the floor, overlapping one another; more worn velvet chairs were pushed side by side; silver trays and ivory knickknacks were strewn around the narrow room.

He leaned the picture against a chair and pushed the long thin couch away from the wall. Pushing the couch against the lower frame of the picture, Paul stepped back to admire the hanging of The Captain. It seemed to him that The Captain was in charge of a tug boat rather than in his rightful place on the bridge of a battleship.

"Well, that's that!" Mrs. Leveler shouted from the dining room. She fumbled through some drawers of the buffet.

"May I stay awhile?" Paul asked. "I'd like to look around, alone. Miss Ottoman said it would be all right."

"Do whatever you like. I got to go shopping anyhow. They won't last long here," she mumbled walking toward the door.

Paul heard the creaking of the loose boards when she crossed the front porch. He watched from the window as she disappeared around the corner of the South Side. Then he hurried to the car and took the light medicine chest from the trunk.

He carried it into the bedroom and placed the chest in a corner of the clothes-closet and withdrew, but an inquiring urge overcame him before locking the door. Reentering, he tried to open the chest, but it was locked. He would never know for sure.

Paul quickly locked the door, placing the key beneath a pillow before leaving.

Walking into the front room occupied by The Captain, Paul noticed the small picture of Johnny on a table. The high arched eyebrows, the pudgy nose, and thin cheeks angered Paul. He felt the forgotten pain shoot through his chest, and then he knew why his childhood friend had meant so much to him. Suddenly he knocked the picture from the table with the back of his hand. The glass shattered when it hit the floor.

He locked the front door of the yellow house walking dejectedly toward the car. Paul was frightened at his discovery, and he swore silently never to see the Ottoman family again...

Christmas

Snow fell in fat flakes. The Westway, half bar, half hotel, gathered the snow around its wide cement walk which encircled the establishment, caught the snow on the high flat roof, and shot chunks of black soot into the crisp air. Judy Anders stopped in front of the half frosted window facing Center Street, tapped on the glass with her leather gloves and waved at the bartender inside. She beat her heavily clothed arms as though a disease lingered on them, and the crusted snow fell to mix with that on the ground. Soon the door opened and Hank Stark was shouting into the thin air. "Hey Judy, come in and have a nip on me."

"No thank you, Hank. Have you seen Leo? He's gone and got the Chris-baas spirit and left his poor Ange in labor at the hospital. Poor thing, she's not well at all, not at all."

"He's not here, Judy. Probably bought 'imself a bottle and hid out. Leo was never the likes to be courting hospitals."

The scrappy looking bartender laughed and disappeared inside. Judy turned in the snow and walked to her car parked in the side lot.

Dag Mercer watched Judy struggle through the snow, slide into the auto's seat, and start the engine. Dag enjoyed watching women, wearing dresses, slip into cars since it afforded an opportunity to see their thighs and sometimes even higher. But Judy Anders shifted her legs inside without a trace of white skin. Once the door was shut, Dag skipped up to the car. "Har, Mrs. Anders. Har, Mrs. Anders!" he shouted.

The car window came down and he leaned toward it.

"Got any wood needin' chopped? Har, Mrs. Anders, got no errands?"

"You've been drinking, Dag."

"Just beer, for holidays."

"You're not old 'nuff to drink, Dag."

"Yes um."

"How old are you?" No one in Clay Town was ever in such a hurry to leave when a laugh could be managed at the expense of Dag.

"Eh, old 'nuff. Old 'nuff, Mrs. Anders."

"And how old would that be, Dag?" The voice broke into giggles from far inside the car.

"Mr. McBridy says I'm eighteen."

"And what follows eighteen, Dag? Do you know? You told me three years ago that you were eighteen."

"That's when Mr. McBridy told me I was that old."

"And after eighteen?" Mrs. Anders inquired.

The alcohol prevented him from talking to the inquisitive woman. In fact, at this moment, Dag didn't much like Mrs. Anders.

"Gotta go."

Mrs. Anders understood and handed him a quarter from the window before driving into the slush-covered street. Dag looked on, gripping the quarter in his big, ungloved right hand. He gasped the crisp air through an open mouth and gazed with emptiness in the direction of the moving vehicle. Dag crossed his heavy engineering boots, pulled at his baseball cap with the C symbol, and spit a mouthful of chewing tobacco into the white snow. His entire body responded in bumps and grinds as he turned and skipped along the path leading to the Westway. Behind, the tobacco left a yellow stain in the snow.

"Well! If it ain't Dag come after his Christmas drink," the General shouted seeing the boy standing silently in the doorway.

"Now don't you be pickin' on the kid, General," Harry O'Brien warned. Harry had finished his heavy Christmas mail route earlier and was taking advantage of his last stop with a beer before dinner. Bill Blake was called the "General" though he had only been a Captain during the Second World War. The name stuck with him because of Bill's boasting that if he had continued with the army, he would have become a general. This was always said in a near stupor, as he later admitted, while working in his blacksmith shop; nevertheless, the name stuck.

"Me? Pick on poor old Dag?" He turned on the bar stool and stared at the spastic gestures of the young man. "Come here, boy, and let the General buy you a drink. Why, he's as good a soldier as the next. Look at 'im! Strong as two bears with 'bout enough brains for one mouse."

Dag started the marvelous energy that set his body swaying and leaping toward the General.

"Now don't you be makin' fun of me, General. I got own money. Can buy self drink if want. I'm old 'nuff too. Ain't I, Hank?"

"Sure you are kid. what'll it be?" Dag stopped at the bar and thought.

"What's he drinking?" Dag pointed.

"The General?"

"Har. General. What's his?"

"Bourbon, my boy. The drink of kings and generals," the heavy man answered.

"I want too."

"That's after my heart," the General slapped Dag on the back.

"Ouch. You mean! I take drink next to Mr. Harry."

Dag moved to the empty bar stool next to the postman. But the General soon followed him.

"Here, I'll pay." The General threw down a dollar.

"Don't want money." Dag loosened the quarter from his fist and it wobbled onto the counter. "See, got own."

"But I'm your pal, boy," the General shouted. "Didn't I help you out last week?"

"How'd you help 'im, General?" Harry asked.

"Well, he came asking me what you should do for a frozen radiator so I told 'im to fill the gas tank with hot stones." The General laughed. "Sure, why not? They do it in wells. But it didn't work in the car, did it Dag? Sorry boy, but since I'm no mechanic, I can be wrong 'bout them things sometimes. I'm never wrong 'bout tempering steel, but the old General can be wrong 'bout those contraptions, even if I have one."

"That was downright mean of you, General." The postman did not like the General when the tall, heavy, bourbon drinker was drunk.

"Dag don't know much 'bout engines, but he wants to learn, an' I heard you spoilt that job with Johnny's filling station for him."

"Now Harry, never you mind." The General laughed. Between gasps, he pounded his fat, white hand on the bar.

"The General's got his own sense of humor. Dag." Harry asked as the laughter passed to giggles, "how did the rocks help? Did they unfreeze the radiator?"

Dag uncovered his head and placed the ball cap over the drink. He began twirling it on top of the glass. Dag felt happy. These were his friends. Even the General wanted to buy him a drink. Dag smiled, tried to speak. Only grunts and giggles wiggled out. This caused more laughter among the men.

Into the mirth, Leonard Angelo staggered to a stool. He did

not cause the laughter to stop, but rather, when the men looked and saw the small body of Leo climbing onto the stool, they broke out again.

"Well, if it ain't Father Time." Hank shouted. "Has she had it yet?"

"A boy, I hope," the General added. "Hope you're man enough to bring men into the world. Wouldn't give all the wars in hell for my boy, Dody. Got to bring men into the world."

"It's not 'im that brings 'em in," Hank said, drawing a beer for Leo. "Better believe he has no say so now. By the way, Leo, Mrs. Anders was looking for you. She was a peeping in here not more'n minutes ago. That old nurse'll be pouncing on you before the night's out."

Leo waved it off, and the men laughed harder. Dag felt unhappy. They had forgotten him. He uncovered his drink and gulped it down.

"She have a hard time?" Leo took the beer in both hands and rested it against his lips. "She been there too long and no baby. What I gonna do?"

The postman walked to Leo's stool and put an arm around his shoulders. "Man, you should be there at the hospital. It ain't good for you to be here. It ain't good to be drinking when your wife's there."

When Harry lost his wife, and the drunkenness of the following day, and the hangover of the day after that, he thought about the early morning coldness. He had been deathly sick — no help to anyone — and now he felt sorry for the small Italian.

"Come off it, Harry!" The General resented the restriction to his fun making. "She'll be okay, then you'll regret not celebrating in the first place. Now me, I'd send Dag over and get the latest news while you relax here, huh Leo? I'll buy you some good beer, some real beer. Hey Harry, got any German stuff left? That's the beer! We fought 'em cross the Rhine and drank all their god-damn beer."

"Don't wanna hear story now," Leo shifted his weight. "Ange, she plenty sick. Labor all night, all morning."

"The General's right," Hank answered wiping a Heineken. "Here, he'll buy you some good beer. Best to buck up. Send Dag over to the hospital."

"No wanna German beer. Give me American beer."

With the mention of his name, Dag had become interested in the conversation and had rushed to the side of Leo, wobbling from one foot to the other.

"Har, Mr. Angelo, Har, Mr. Angelo, I go see 'bout Misses. She no better, I come tell you."

Leo waved him away, but the General saw humor in Dag's eagerness. He took the boy gently by the neck and led him to the record machine, standing idle in a corner.

"So you want to help, hey?"

"Har, har, Mr. Angelo might give Dag a tip."

"Well, here's a dollar." The General reached into his pocket and drew out a crumpled bill. "Now you go up to the hospital and you just ask if Mrs. Angelo dropped it in the basket yet. You hear, has she dropped it in the basket yet?"

The General noted the confused expression on the overhanging forehead of the boy. "You know what Dropsie is?"

"Dropsie?" Dag repeated slowly. "Dropsie?"

"It's a sickness women get. Mrs. Angelo's suffering from it. That's why Leo's so low." The General pointed to the Italian at the bar.

"She drop it in the basket yet?" Dag repeated to himself assuring his benefactor that he knew how to carry a message.

"You git now."

"Har, General, I tell 'em. Drink first." Dag fought the grip of the General and struggled toward the bar. "Drink is mine."

"No, no, Dag. You git. That drink'll be there when you get back. Hurry now."

The General pushed Dag toward the door and the boy reluctantly reentered the snow covered world outside. After Dag had departed, the General turned to face the men staring with wonder at him.

"Now that's all fixed Leo. Dag'll report to you here. He's a good lad but a little slow."

This speech was unnecessary since they knew about Dag's mental retardation.

"No, no," Leo shouted. "Me go. Wrong to stay here." He staggered around the bar and disappeared through the back door.

"Just as well. He'd be a damper now that he's pent up 'bout the baby." The General did not resume his seat, but instead, stood in front of Dag's drink.

"Hey, did I ever tell you 'bout the time we put alum in the Sarg's drink? He drank it right down and we got him to whistling. What a sight, I tell ya. What a sight. He just stood there after that whistling, with his mouth all screwed up like this."

The General squeezed his lips together until he was talking through a tiny hole in his mouth. Then laughter opened his mouth wide again. When he stopped, the General slammed his fist on the bar.

"Got any alum, Harry?"

"Wouldn't be a trick you was thinking 'bout playin' on Dag?"

"You're goddamn right I am."

Harry giggled and let the empty leather sack fall from his shoulder.

"General, you've got a stunt for everybody for every hour of the day. But poor Dag gets most of 'em thrown his way."

The General raised his hand for silence. "Just wait 'till Dag goes wobbling into the hospital and asks if Mrs. Angelo has dropped the kid into a basket yet."

"Dropped it in a basket?" The two men became puzzled.

"Sure, I told the kid she had the Dropsie and he's gonna ask if she dropped it in a basket yet."

There was another period of laughter. After awhile the postman and bartender joined in.

Dag never returned to the drink at the Westway. After Mrs. Simpson, the head nurse, had shouted at him until he ran from the hospital and could see her no more, Dag began to realize that the General had played another trick on him. Dag entered the woods below the hospital and sat on a fallen log. He felt the wet from the snow seep through his green trousers. His humiliation was too great to take much notice of the wetness. He hung his head and cried, repeating, "Har, har, I don't know what dropsie is. They told me to ask if she dropped it in a basket yet. Me sorry, Mrs. Simpson. I no do it 'gain."

His head bounced with each sob. There were squirrels playing above Dag, but in the late evening Dag did not notice.

That night it was Christmas Eve. The snow started to fall at six o'clock and continued for an hour. The falling flakes touched and remained on the abandoned Christmas trees bunched in lots on the South Side. These green lifeless sentinels were the only guards to the narrow streets.

Leo walked aimlessly out of darkness into a lighted street — into the falling flakes — his wide eyes conveying stupor, his tightly shut mouth betraying loneliness within. He walked slowly at first touch of light, then his thin legs spread the land between them, seeming to hurry again into the night and anxious to be swallowed by darkness. His shadowed red eyes searched the street for comfort. There was none — only the speckled Christmas trees, the mingled dirt and snow of the gutter, and the darkness around him. A newspaper, caught on the wind, fluttered its pale white past him.

Leo passed churches, empty of souls, homes, dirty and blank. He heard the wet wind sweep against tin roofs. Then he stopped at the corner of Golding Street and tried to gather his collar about him.

"Why you no speak?" He shook a bare fist at the trees standing idle in the vacant lot across the street.

"Why you no speak? She dead! I tell you. Dead! Dead! Dead! Dead! She no come back!"

Leo rushed the Christmas trees in anger. They toppled as he ran up and down the paths between them, waving, pushing, pulling. Exhausted, he slumped to the ground near the tiny shack.

Leo stared into the darkness of the shack and saw the letter "C". It seemed to bounce out at him. Leo quickly crossed himself. The C carried forward until the awkward stride of Dag met the light. The boy stared at Leo with a bottle poised behind his back. "Har there! You crazy? Trees my fort. Har, you knock down."

Leo, frightened by the first image of Dag, now let his heavy head fall against his chest.

"Har, Mr. Angelo. How Mrs. Angelo? Dag remembered not to ask about dropsie. "She better, har?"

"Give me drink." The Italian grabbed at the bottle which he knew by instinct Dag had hidden behind him. Before Dag could answer, Leo had swallowed long drinks. Dag only watched as the other man's Adam's apple bounced. Then Mr. Angelo threw the bottle and hit the slow moving Dag on the shoulder.

"I kill you!"

Leo did not want to kill Dag. He wanted to kill the god inside him who had the power to kill and create. So Dag stood before him embellished with the letter C on Christ's eve, the letter C on his ball cap standing for the Cleveland Indians. It was difficult for Leo to hit Dag at first. Soon, with each renewed action of his arm, it became easy to throw flesh against flesh. Finally, the stunned boy, happy with the hits, making him forget the pain of Mrs. Simpson's words, fell onto the snow beside the shack.

Leo straightened at the sounds from the Catholic Church bells. He glanced at his skinned knuckles and shook his head. "I no wanna kill you, Dagburt."

Then his legs were working along the snow covered street again. He stopped on the bridge separating the shacks of the South Side with downtown, glanced into the icy water and hurried on. He stopped again before the lights of the Westway, reached into his pocket and brought out a few silver coins. He ran up the cold path and disappeared into the warmth of lights.

Down the street the dirt smudged newspaper took flight again on a small wind and flew smoothly over the snow. Suddenly it was pushed through the rail of the bridge onto the icy water below. The paper swam silently upon the dark water for a moment then was drawn into the water's icy grip...

Soon it would be 1954.

Part IV
SPRING

Covered Bridge

Dag Mercer stretched his two legs across the gutter and watched Dorothy Wilson approach him on the curb of Grant Street. At first he believed she had stuffed pillows beneath the spring dress, but Dag, thinking, remembered Mrs. Latty, who was uncommonly large in the middle, had a baby the day after he saw her. Dorothy was a mother in his mind, and he respected her not knowing why. He arose as she passed and tipped his red baseball cap with the C icon representing the Cleveland Indians.

"Har, Mrs. Wilson. Help you?"

"No thanks, Dag. I'm going into the drug store."

Dag felt happy that Dorothy was in a motherly way. She looked funny, but Dag would have been the last to laugh even though he wanted to laugh. Her tent-like body seemed to sway more gently, more gracefully with the acquired pouch. Dag thought her lovely. Dorothy smiled at Dag, then entered her father-in-law's pharmacy.

"Morning Dorothy," Mr. Wilson hurried to his daughter-in-law. "It's a wonderful day, yes? Spring popped just in time, yes?"

"Yes it did, Mr. Wilson."

"Dad. Dad to you, Dorothy. You're looking a little pink, yes? What does Doctor Gerom say?"

"It's overdue, that's all. It's just overdue." Dorothy leaned on the counter and rested the baby inside her.

"But Dorothy, it's a God-send, I tell you. We've got to be thankful it's late."

Dorothy understood her father-in-law's concern since she had felt the first regrets of unmarried motherhood before Jimmy acted with honor. How the father hoped for legitimacy. But Dorothy knew that the baby's record would be marked. Dorothy, feeling the hot and cold of spring, did not care. Within her there was some secret god telling her about all the secrets of the past; revealing mysteries of ark rites; speaking tongues of forgotten civilizations, and Dorothy was happy and sad.

"Where's Jimmy?"

"Your husband is a busy beaver. I sent him, just this moment, to deliver an order to Mrs. Willomenia, yes. Poor dear woman, out there all by herself. My, my, you're lucky though. Nothing is going to make things difficult for a Wilson, yes? Is the apartment comfortable?"

"Oh yes, Mr. Wilson. Only I have so little to do."

"Nothing to do? Why you have to look after our little son, heh? 'Course, Mrs. Wilson feels badly that you two didn't move in with us. Large house, yes, and you'd be ever more comfortable and safe, but Jimmy has his ways, yes."

"I'd like to have this prescription filled, Mr. Wilson." Dorothy shoved the crumpled white paper under the pharmacist's eye glasses to distract his thoughts. "Doctor Gerom said it was important."

"Oh yes, these things are quite important, yes, but you should have had Jimmy carry it to you."

Outside of town, Jimmy projected only his thoughts into the future. His languid spring-heavy body dangled its legs listlessly over the side. The Wilson Pharmacy pick-up truck rested a few feet from the covered bridge. Jimmy sat in the freshness of sunlight, staring into the cool dark of the wooden tunnel. At first he thought about Dorothy while wiggling his legs above the stream, but then the creaking wood turned his thoughts forward and he saw the bridge, stripped of its wood, replaced with steel and rivets, and he picked a splinter from the large board beside him, and studied it as if the splinter held the mystery of his fears. But the wood crumbled beneath his fingers.

"Not safe, but it's so pretty," he said. "I don't want to cross you, but I've got too, don't I?" He questioned the bridge then waited for an answer. "Much as I like you, you got to go 'cause you won't hold the weight of that pick-up."

Jimmy wondered how long the stream had existed before the bridge then he wondered how many cars had passed over it.

"Must of been plenty since Mrs. Willomenia has to get back and forth to town."

He threw a pebble into the stream and the moving water gulped up the weight.

"Maybe I can cross on foot and walk up to the Willomenia place and not take the truck across it." This thought pleased Jimmy. He did not understand why.

Sure, I can cross on foot and walk to her place. It's only a mile or so, he thought staring at a broken board. He didn't fear to walk across the bridge, but neither did he stir, rather, he gazed into its cool darkness. The small sun light on the other side met him. But there would be the rotten wood to cross, he thought. The sun reflected from the yellow steel of the truck. Jimmy wanted to drive it across the bridge to the Willomenia place, but he knew the bridge would not hold the weight. More than that, he did not want to take the truck farther into the hills, far outside Clay Town, so he sat and thought. To Jimmy, the new, yellow truck looked ugly there. It did not belong.

But he would be late for dinner. Dorothy would worry. The child, not yet a child, would grumble and miss the daily pat he gave her stomach. She would call Dad at the store a few minutes past noon and learn that the son had taken the better half of a morning to deliver a single package into the woods. Jimmy seized a larger pebble and threw it violently at the stream below. Water climbed in wet fragments.

"Late, late, late, late. I can be late just once if I want!" Jimmy shouted into the cold darkness of the bridge.

"She can just wait!"

He felt ashamed at his anger He thought the bridge as some mysterious self which he had involuntarily expressed.

"You know, don't you?" He had completed the break from human thoughts to verbal protests at a bridge. He could not stop.

"You're like the woods 'cause you know and I haven't talked to the woods since those times me and Dorothy..." Jimmy stopped, knowing that not even the bridge could know his thoughts about that.

"Well, you do know. And I never want to go back. I just want to sit here and guard you in the hot sun."

The young man laughed. His voice echoed through the walls of the bridge.

"You mock me!" he shouted, straightening himself. "You laugh back at me 'cause I said I'd get away and I didn't." There was only the creaking wood for an answer.

"Maybe I'm better off, hey? You get to come down 'cause you can't even hold cars anymore let alone trucks like mine, yeah, trucks like mine 'cause they are mine. I'll own a whole fleet of 'em and knock all the bridges down and tear up your wood! That's what I'll do!"

There were birds singing near Jimmy, perched above the overhead bridge. Their singing, once loved by Jimmy, became a discordant and shrill sound to his ears. He grasped a hand full of rocks and began to throw them at the bridge so near. He spied a robin and hit it squarely. The bird attempted to fly away, but instead, fell down into the stream. Jimmy did not see the bird fall into the water, but he knew it would die.

"I hate these backward woods. I hate this dilapidated bridge, and here I am, talking to 'em like they're real! I hate you! I hate you! You got to come down!"

Jimmy ran to the bright yellow truck and climbed into the cab. He stepped heavily on the accelerator and the steel and rubber met the wood and nails with weight and speed. Boards rattled and creaked beneath him, but Jimmy drove fast through the darkness of the bridge. Now, the engine had revived him. He bounced in the seat and laughed. Once over the bridge he felt ashamed and slowed the truck.

At the town hospital, sitting in brick stability on a remote hill, Dorothy pushed Mary Wilson into the world at 7:45 p.m. that evening. Mr. and Mrs. Wilson congratulated their son on having a fine baby, on having a fine wife. They felt proud, but Jimmy only answered, "I am happy... and sad."

The Urge

Joe Manner wasn't born too late, at least he didn't think so. He left Clay Town one Friday night with five dollars in his pocket, a chip on his shoulder, and the wisdom of fifteen years. He saw the world, first in the Navy, later as a merchant marine, and much later as a railroad hobo. Then one Friday, when a red and yellow twilight came over the spring hills, he returned with two friends, met along the long evasive route.

Joe esteemed himself higher than a mere bum, reserving the title, hobo, to mean a free traveler, resembling ancient troubadours he had read about somewhere — he hadn't remembered where, but that made no difference — in books he had treasured but had forgotten when. Perhaps it was in the Navy when he began reading about exotic places and the mystical names they connoted since Joe hardly ever visited them — being aboard a destroyer; perhaps he had read about them before leaving Clay Town, in the thin-walled school with a pot belly stove — Hong Kong, Nile, Katmandu, the Alps. Later he visited the places and they lived up to the books — Paris, Madrid, San Francisco. Joe was free, and a free traveler cannot stop long.

The sojourn to Clay Town came in the night to Joe. Traveling the rails out of Columbus, he smelled the Midwest, knowing this was home. Broken corn stalks and pumpkins seen once a year and harvest moons and frost beneath barefoot feet. He told his friends about Clay Town, leaping to his feet in the wooden rail car as boyhood tales grew in exaggeration, and the men listened and wanted to see the town where Joe had split the shackles of youth. The train sped them toward the sloping hills, away from the flat lands of Columbus, east into the glaciers' last resting place.

So the three men tripped across the cracked pavement of Clay Town at twilight, heading for the long, steep hill behind plant number three because Joe knew that his relatives would still live there. Mr. Wilson watched them pass and wondered what foreigners were dominating the country. Dag Mercer spoke to them on the outskirts, thinking Joe a night worker at the plant. Three shadows made their way up the path behind the factory merging to the night. Slim stopped to spit.

"Jesus Christ, man, that ain't them factories you told us 'bout, huh? Why that looks like something from Chicago's backside." Slim sniffed the smoky air, allowing his words to resound against the night, then walked on.

"They're the same factories I left, Goddamn it! Nothing changed." Joe Manner puffed the cigarette expertly, knowing it was the last of a pack. "No difference, I see."

"Got any ass here?" Rags asked being the youngest of the trio. "Goddamn, I've not seen a broad since that city up the line."

"Always talkin' ain't ya, Rags?" Slim detested Rag's preoccupation. It was cause of constant trouble.

"Leave 'im alone, Slim. He can look all he wants."

"Look, yeah, but Christ, he don't need to go pullin' them tricks of his. Not with no sense he can't. We're gonna leave you get out of 'em scrapes alone some of these days, ain't we, Joe?"

Joe Manner did not answer looking at the rock stumps around them. He tramped across the decaying limestone foundation, stood on the moss-covered bricks then turned and lifted his head.

"This is the place."

"Guess your relatives moved on, huh, Joe?"

"They sure didn't leave nuttin' standing," Rags added inspecting the weeds.

The deserted worn farm house had stood snug against the hill. Its apron of plowed fields running onto the sewer pipe factory land was now replaced by weeds growing tall in the last specks of day.

"There's light up there," Rags pointed farther up the hill.

"Bet they can tell us where they lit out to. Sure is plenty cold 'nuff."

The three men started for the tiny lights. Joe, being leader of the hobo-gang, led. They reached the lights peeking through trees growing in the spring weather. Joe knocked. It was not a house. It was not a mere shelter. Someone obviously lived in this shack, so Joe Manner knocked and they waited.

The wooden door opened and J.C. Pulton poked his head out of the light toward them, staring with wild drink into the shadows, expecting to let the devil into his abode, hoping for the charm of youth, mumbling between the parched lips of age and wine.

"Tar and tendation, who's there? Name yourselves before I cut your guts! Name quickly out there!"

"I'm Joe Manner and I just returned to stop in at the Manner farm down there, but it's not there, huh?"

The round pouch of J.C. Pulton pushed forward until it blocked the narrow doorway in bouncing fits of laughter.

"You're ten years late, fella. The Manners 'er long gone. Jake, that your cousin?" He went on without an answer. "He got put up in the booby hatch, but tar and tendation, trip in and spend a drink with me. It's my land now and I'm beholding to any Manner since it was Jake who left it me."

The stomach disappeared and the three men stepped into the two room shack.

"Not much is it?" J. C. Pulton flopped into a chair at an unstable kitchen table standing in the middle of the room. He poured himself another drink.

"But I can call it home. I see you're men like me, guys that ain't 'fraid of common worlds, that chew their breakfast and meet the day with tight muscles."

The three men stared with bewilderment at J.C. Pulton, then at the wine on the table. J.C. Pulton was drunk, but he was friendly.

"Come, join the last of us men in a toast to us, huh, fellow men?"

"Sure, fella," Rags' eyes shifted around the room, his pupils constricting, studying, calculating all around him. He took the lone seat beside the fat man and eyed the port before him.

"Get some chairs from the bedroom, men. Get out of the cold and warm your bellies." J.C. Pulton pointed to the small, iron oil stove with a can of oil on top of it.

"Good wine, good company, fat fire, and my feet with stockings, that's what I call life, huh, men?"

"It's a damn sight better'n we expected." Joe answered returning with a chair and a stool. The stool rocked with one short leg as Slim sat on it.

"We been traveling on the line for a month now. This here is the first real warm place we've been at since, well, since, since where, Slim?"

"Iowa maybe?"

"I'm J. C. Pulton," the fat man proclaimed under the spell of drink.

"Well J.C., this is Slim and Rags, and I'm Joe."

"Got any last names, men?"

"Nope. Lost 'em when we hit the road." Slim rocked on the stool and was happy.

"Just as well, can't 'member last names to save my soul. Real men shouldn't have last names. Last names give men responsibilities and tear down manhood. Pretty soon them with last names become old women. They putter 'round shops, gossipin' and carrying on like old maid shopkeepers. A shame it is to give men last names. Ruins 'em."

"You got a last name, J.C. You don't seem to have responsibilities?" The metaphysical look of Rags met the red eyes of J. C. Pulton.

"Kid, I got responsibilities to myself, or I'd be flyin' 'round like you'ens. Besides, I keep a wife and they'd throw me in the can if I didn't pay for her each month. But tar and tendation, drink up. I got plenty of wine even if I got a last name.

"You work down there at that factory, don't you?" Joe remembered the sweat of summer and the clay dust clinging to him.

J. C. Pulton nodded his head and drank, offering the wine into chalices, or rather, three cracked coffee cups which Rags took from the lone cupboard.

So the men drank, and later, J.C. Pulton, in a wine happy mood, tripped to the rear of the cabin and uncovered more wine. The men, united in manly fellowship, drank and talked until their desires twisted the thoughts and pulled each to his own pleasure, crashing the unity and sending each man into separate, isolated worlds, shelling and stamping their thoughts with single adventures to pleasure.

Rags, sitting straight, his blond hair twisted and knotted, began to feel the tingle inside his groin.

"I say old man, you got any houses of pleasure in this town?"

"He means whore houses, J.C." Slim added.

"You fellows in need of physical comfort?" J.C. was hurt.

"You're tired of my company, are you? Yeah, men stuff, talking for sake of talkin' and being together, never lasts. We get together and just as soon as we talk, women come in and dirty up the gatherin'. But we got several of 'em houses here."

"Hey Joe, fella, how 'bout us cuttin' out for one?"

"Money?"

"Just a couple of bucks. We'll just look, won't we, Slim!"

"Now none of your filthy stunts tonight." Slim, slumped on the stool, craved flesh, but he knew, looking through his tall body, that Rags couldn't stop with just having a woman. No, the kid had to have trouble around him, women and trouble, and it made Slim sick to think of the past tricks Rags had found for pleasure. But Slim craved flesh. The gathering of men had ended. Now there was silence and the craving of women. J. C. Pulton drank his drink unconcerned, now, with the men around him. Joe pulled out his wallet and counted money.

"Thirty dollars. Boys. That's all we can afford. Sorry 'bout that. We should be able to get jobs in Pennsylvania for awhile and pick up another car."

"Ain't you comin', Joe?" Slim, rubbing his partially bald head, asked.

"I'm tired, and J.C. says we can sleep here, so I'm gonna sack out."

Rags and Slim stumbled toward Clay Town with a map J.C. had drawn and Joe talked and drank with the fat man.

"It's the kid in 'em. I used to be the same way. I still am, I guess." Joe drank his drink and remembered cold days with passion's sweaty heat.

"Funny how this world's put together," J. C. was a happy philosopher.

"Everything is so simple but everybody keeps making it out to be complicated. I say it's simple in comparison to the world but it's not simple to us 'cause we're not big 'nuff to get it all.

We try to make it complicated, sit back and just make things more mixed up, but tar and tendation, them two has an itch and they want to scratch it. Make it all simple, like a lone man and see the world in him."

Joe Manner felt the meaning of J.C.'s words.

"But what happens when you put a woman with 'em, the man I mean? First of all, you're taking on unnatural products with women. Women, or at least what we call women, have been so corrupted and made themselves over so much, that they ain't nothing like the world. So you got to take man first and throw out women, at least, her false things, then you'd have just plain simple things left.

They were happy to be away from J.C. The blow-fish as Rags called him.

In the room the women come and go, speaking soft, tinkling laughter of the body, and Rags, gripping the shoulder of Slim for support, watched through pinched eyes at the flowing laughter.

"Big boobs, ripe as mistletoe on Christmas limbs, and here we stand, hey, my brave buddy, Slim, waiting before the door of juiced seas."

"You're drunk, Rags. No trouble from you, now." Slim emphasized the warning by a stiff punch at Rags' side. Rags stiffened sharply.

"Walking piss pots of pleasure. Look at bobbling bodies, ripe for haying!"

Some kind of a party was in progress and Slim helped his friend stumble onto a couch, becoming part of the moving yellowish dream. Slim didn't trust Rags in this kind of mood. He didn't like Rags when he was like this.

The youth pinched a girl beside him. His pinch left a red welt on her teat. She screamed and slapped Rags.

"Sick white body bouncing with pleasure."

"You can't do that to me!"

"He didn't mean no harm, lady."

Mrs. Gray advanced to the new girl covering her smarting teat.

At the decrepit house J.C. Pulton drank the wine and continued, pouring red into the chalice. "And the men are simple. They're just babies without harms. Oh, sure, they'd kill ya, but that, in the end, ain't really harm. Nothing what women can do. Why, a woman can chew ya up, spit ya out, and still ya'd have the same looks and feel and smell, but there wouldn't be nothing there. Now death is natural 'cause it let's your body go. You rot and crawl up inside the earth, but tar and tendation, a woman after killin' ya, goes on to embalm ya in walking death."

Joe was tired and drunk, but he felt the meaning of the words. He didn't care if he understood. Joe sat and felt the words.

"Women that we're talking 'bout ain't all in dresses. The men that are killed are 'em, the ones that suck on sour teats are 'em, and so you can't take and look under a dress to see which is which. It's in here that ya know." J. C. Pulton pounded his middle, between the heart and his protruding stomach. "In here! In here!"

At the whore house across town trouble stirred in a boiling caldron.

"I should have been a pair of ragged claws, huh, Slim?" Rags swung on the girl sitting beside him and bit her neck. Mrs. Gray stood tall and yellow over them. Slim wanted to go into the night, out of the yellow. He wanted to leave Rags to his self inflicted punishment.

"You got to go!" Slim nudged Rags as Mrs. Gray advanced.

"Want I whip 'em for you, mother Bitch?" Slim asked.

"Have the devil inside me and he's dancing on pin curls tonight!"

"I'll get 'im out, lady. He's a friend."

"I have money and the devil's inside me!" Slim stood. "Let him out, whore!"

Joe felt the years confirm J. C.'s words. He smiled. The words became hollow at the lips of J.C. Pulton. He hadn't lived them. He was dreaming, and Joe knew he was dreaming because he, Joe Manner, had lived them. He felt the degrading effects of living those words — the sad heart, the empty dirty pockets, a full soul but no one to share it with so Joe sat, smiled, listened and felt the years jerk inside him.

"Men ain't men unless they're men in here. I found that out! I was startin' to follow so I left her and now she wants my money 'cause that's all she can get."

As J.C. rambled in his living room, Rags reacted with drunkenness at the whore house. "I don't think that they'll sing to me. No one sings to me, upon my soul, you sing, whore and make me crawl straight." Rags clutched at her bare shoulder climbing the steps, turning to see if they sang, but everything was yellow. He blinked his eyes and allowed her to lead. At the top of the stairs he turned again.

"Look people in purple, I'm the devil in white." He pushed the whore away from him, perhaps not knowing that she must go down, perhaps knowing and seeing all the time she must tumble the stairs; laughing and swaying until he made a swan dive, landing on top of her.

They were scared then angry. The yellow shouts made Slim

run. He stopped only when reaching the door of the shack wanting any light but yellow, sweating and cold.

Inside, Joe asked, "Rags, what happened?"

"She's dead."

"And money?"

"Gone."

"Christ, we got to run. They'll be after us. You sure she didn't move?"

"Broken neck."

"Thanks J. C. You're a real friend."

"Stay here. They'll never find ya."

"I should have known. Coming back was bad." Joe shook his head then ran.

The fat man waved at the shadows going, then he passed out...

Blacksmith Pond

They hunched in the dusty corner, watching red sparks, smelling hot, burning iron and stale chewing tobacco, hearing the sharp slams of the hammer, while the light of day sunk below the window sill. The General, not really a general but a burly white-haired blacksmith, brought his hammer again to the horseshoe resting on the anvil, held by long forceps. He raised it again, spit into the fire and struck home. The spit sizzled and disappeared into the flames beside him. The General swung around and dunked hot iron into a large barrel of water. Dody, his son, and Dody's friend, Grover McFadden, watched the steam rise and the water bubble from their hovel in the corner. Dody was waiting for the shoe to be twisted before asking the question, but the General, anticipating his son's request, spoke first.

"Dody, you flesh-haired son of a…git me 'nother off the shelf."

Dody, preoccupied with the best method by which to advance the financial question, ducked beneath the halters, hanging from rafters, and took the horseshoe without speaking. Handing it to his father, Dody faded into the corner beside Grover McFadden. The General had begun to heat the new iron when Grover nudged Dody. The youth, jumping to his feet, paced nearer the General.

"Pa?" The General did not look up from his work. "Pa, can I have a couple of bucks?"

"Loose change, heh?" The General saw Dody, patting the horse, by shifting his eyes upward, but he did not raise his head.

"Couple of bucks is all, pa."

"Girls?"

"Yeah."

"Where you takin' 'em? New York?"

"Now Mr. Blake, we got dates for the prom." Grover had promised Dody his help. He found himself beside the hunk of anvil.

"You see, a senior prom ain't nutten to sneeze at. Sure, it costs, but all the kids go. It's... it's a tradition like shoeing horses." Grover propped his foot on the stained cuspidor and readied himself to talk, but the General stopped him.

"Hell Grover, you two don't need to crowd me. I'm not that old. Fact, I can tell you some stories 'bout my prom that'd set ya dancin', and better yet, some real lively ones 'bout them dances in the cellars of Germany when we was fightin' our way through."

Dody and Grover had heard the war stories and their attention had been aroused with the General's sympathy toward their dilemma. Dody spoke first. "How much can I have?"

"How 'bout twenty? That do you?" The General pulled the iron from the fire and inspected it.

"Great Gods!" Dody stuck his hands in the khaki army jacket, not knowing what to do with them.

"Course, you're gonna drive the car?"

"Can I?"

"Hell yes. No time at all you'll be in the army and you'll have responsibilities with vehicles, so damn well start learning now. You takin' that Elsie Grazio? Seeing a lot of her lately h'ain't you?"

"Well yeah."

"Got to watch yourself when playing with fire. If you go knockin' her up, the army won't be takin' kindly to you."

"Well, yeah." Dody had nothing further to say, but he felt obligated to listen, considering the twenty dollars recently awarded him.

"So watch yourself in the back seat." Dody had followed Grover to the door, which had shut out blackness. The General, paying no attention to his work, sunk the hot iron in the water and the steam and sizzling water followed the two boys into the night.

The shop overlooked a large bottom land which became flooded each spring, which caused it to be called Blacksmith Pond by the townspeople. One end of the bottom was used as a football practice field by St. Mary's. Another section, near the creek, had been converted into a softball field. It offered Grover and Dody many evenings of pleasure while they skipped along the higher ground. Their walks through Blacksmith Pond, named after the General's outmoded but thriving shop, had become important to the youths since Dody found a half-full bottle of whiskey in the creek waters. Grover persuaded Dody to hide the bottle on the bank. Now, after the successful money venture, they made their way down to the hidden bottle and a package of cigarettes.

"That settles that, Grover!" Dody spoke out of the night. "You got to come with me."

"But damn, this is my big chance with Mary. You know she'll probably loosen up that night and I don't want to have no one 'round to mess things up."

"You promised, Grover. Besides, if you ain't got inta Mary's pants by now, you ain't never gonna get in 'em."

"What d'ya mean? No one's got her yet?"

"Look, Grover, she's just takin' you for a ride."

Grover MacFadden stopped on a small hill. "Why's she actin' like that for?"

"'Cause she thinks she's got you. Elsie's pullin' the same stuff with me. They all do it. Like, they think you're their future husband so they make believe they're virgins. Ain't seen it fail yet."

"What?" Grover flapped his arms and flopped on the soft sandy ground.

"What in God's name give girls their brains! Hey they like it like us, don't they?"

"Come on," Dody waved to Grover who could not see him. "Let's get a drink and celebrate the ole man's big heart."

"Now the way I see it is that if they like it as much as we do, why do they have to hold out?" Grover continued talking while resting on his back, his thin knees higher than his body.

Dody pretended to walk a tight rope across the high ground between puddles left by recent flooding. Finally he reached his destination, a smooth, grassy spot near the creek, which was high enough to keep off the muddy waters. Tonight it was occupied. The lights of Clay Town were hardly discernable when Dody drew near. The two were older, Dody thought, and resting on the high ground. He ran quickly back to Grover, who was still reproaching himself but far enough away as not to disturb the couple.

"Hey you freak," Dody whispered. "You're missing som'thin'. I think some guy's 'bout to lay Jinny Pin."

"Who?"

"Jinny Pin," Dody slapped Grover in the arm and motioned him to follow. "The Pin store, you know, the department store up town."

"The old maid! I got to see this!"

The boys crept around the puddles toward the high ground almost hidden by tall weeds. They approached and crouched low to spy on the unaware couple.

186

"It would be a Christian sin to come here for just that, Jinny, my pearl."

"Harry, you animal! Do you think I brought you here for that?"

"Ain't no harm in being a man is there?"

"Harry, there's a large gap between an ordinary man and a gentleman."

"And would a gentleman be courting this, bringin' him near a smelly creek, promising him all kinds of forbidden fruits, and then tellin' 'im 'tain't proper to be makin' love to somebody who needs makin' love to?"

"Perhaps a gentleman would understand. Perhaps he could see the beauty of this night."

"Now don't be poetrying me, Jinny. You had one notion and it ain't makin' words pretty."

Jinny rose to go, but suddenly she was pulled to Harry's side with the sounds of her dress being ripped and the soft silk sounds of nylons rubbing, then the panting of them both.

"He's gonna rape 'er." Grover whispered to Dody. "Maybe we should stop 'im?"

"Shut up. Can't ya see, she wants him to. You was just talkin' 'bout girls likin' it, well, here's one that's hot."

The boys watched and listened and the sounds were confused. The splashing of water found their ears. Grover raised his head to see the long legs of Jinny beneath Harry O'Brien, the mail carrier, dangling in the creek as he panted above her body. With the increasing breath of the mailman, the legs splashed harder until the youths, hidden near by, felt small drops hit their faces. The mud stuck to their cool faces. Grover wondered why she, undressed in the cool evening of spring, could splash her legs purposely in water. Then the splashing ceased, and Grover, once again raising his head, saw the two become one in the night. Dody leaned close to Grover's ear and whispered. "Well, guess you got your baptism tonight, huh?" The voices met them again across the field.

"You okay?"

"Refreshed."

"That's a helleva answer," Harry said rising and dressing. "And why this trip when you got a bed back at the store?"

Jinny did not move. Her legs sunk into the slow moving stream.

"Harry, I feel pregnant with happiness!"

"What's that?" Harry was kneeling. "It's the cold ground that makes you talk silly."

"No. I'm pregnant with your joy. Don't you feel that way? Don't you feel that you have traveled in a different world, if not for a moment, drunk and staggering?"

"Don't ya, be carryin' on so," Harry began dressing again and Jinny became silent. "Don't be carryin' on like this or I'm through with ya."

Another silence came and passed as Jinny splashed the water.

"Dress yourself, Jinny."

She wiggled on the ground and the two youths saw her fully clothed when Harry pulled her up after a moment's wiggling. They walked back to Clay Town leaving the youths in silence.

Dody automatically climbed onto the high ground and dug for the hidden bottle. Grover followed slowly, thinking. He approached Dody who was wiping off the dirt.

"That's the way it should be."

"Sure," Dody answered taking a drink. "That's the way it'll be when we get out of school. Then the girls don't care 'bout savin' themselves. Then, it's different."

They smelled the dampness of night and the pond, talked, drank, and decided to leave for town, the lights, and girls. The smell of Blacksmith Pond lingered with them, the wet, misty smell of swamp, but it soon left them as they approached the lights...

The Vet

"What are governments but political whore houses. What are queens but professional whores. What are statesmen and presidents but pimps. What are great men? Huh, let me answer that! They're blood thirsty animals who repress enough of their beastly blood to dominate the weaker, and they have a magnetic needle pointing in the sole direction of power; if it be blood seeping war or a million deaths in a pithy test tube, you'll see kid, no man is famous unless he's a bastard of the whore house along the way, and no one gets ahead unless he buries a few rotten corpses along the way. We're all alike, don't forget that! Oh, a lot of us don't have enough of the animal left to gulp up others, but we'd like to, that's why we attend football games, gladiators killin' each other, and that's why we climb mountains, and enlist in wars, and watch murder movies on television. It's not just the queens and statesmen who belong to the whore house of beasts, no it's the queers who are women turned inside out, and whiskey dreamers who are shells of the past, and school teachers who are impotent stools, smelling of garbage dumped from the whore house. The whole world is a bed pan. But mind you, it's fertile because the flow spreads on the fields and makes things grow and prosper. I don't have a thing against the queens or statesmen, or fame seekers, or queers, or old maid school teachers wearing men's belts, because they're in it together. That's what makes life so beautiful because from those bed pans come the giant trees of earth, and don't you forget it. Next time you pass a queen or a queer just remember that. They pulled themselves up from the whore house bed and made themselves, made the whore house pay..."

The telephone interrupted the doctor's soliloquy. The gray haired veterinarian sunk back in the swivel chair, puffed his cheeks and let out a stream of air before answering the ring. "Doctor Rider's animal hospital."

Betty Gray's eyes, saucer shaped from the puzzlement of the soliloquy, gazed at Doctor Rider. She smoothed her tweed skirt, brushed her black hair, and listened. Betty had sought out the doctor because he had been a father to her before she left Clay Town to attend the girl's school in Cleveland. Her confession was made with the sincerity of a nun to a priest. The doctor's talk shamed her and surprised her. She wanted sympathy. Instead, she had become involved in the Doctor's complex philosophy, neither understanding nor accepting. Now she could not take her eyes off the German doctor in astonishment.

Doctor Rider placed the telephone on the hook and wheeled around to face Betty. "I'm sorry," he said knowing her present wonderment. "I've had quite a few prostitutes in this office. They always seem to come to me. God only knows why. Maybe it's because I can play with their sin-sides rather than what other men do. I don't know, but I told you my views, thinking it would help you accept this Goddamn world with indifference. Maybe I wanted to show you that you're not so different from the rest of the phonies who drive big cars and own banks. You work harder and get less."

Betty nodded and Doctor Rider continued.

"You left here a sweet girl not knowing that your mother ran a whore house. I knew then that you'd become one. Don't ask me why or how I knew. I just knew. So it's no surprise to me that you came tonight."

"I don't want to give it up, Doctor Rider. Don't tell me I

must. I haven't worked since coming home, but I'm miserable. Momma just keeps me locked up in her home, and now..."

"How can you continue now?" Doctor Rider enjoyed picking his nose, but it bothered clients.

"I'll go away again. I can always work in Columbus or Cleveland or even Chicago."

"What'll you do with the baby?"

"That's why I've come here. Can you take it?"

Doctor Rider's feet hit the floor. He leaned far out of the oak swivel chair, jutting his large red nose toward Betty. He began chewing his nails.

"God almighty, you can't do that! I'm a bachelor. What I mean to say is that a baby needs a mother." He began picking, probing his nose nervously.

"There's a breakdown in society which cannot be justified with dual duties..."

"I don't know what you're talking about," Betty interrupted. "All I know is that you're a good man and you've always treated me with kindness, and that if I ever had a father I would like him to be you. So why shouldn't I leave my baby with you?"

"What will your mother say?"

"She needn't know."

"But she will."

"Then why don't you marry her? You know, doctor, you've been having an affair with her all these years. That's why I knew it was safe telling you why I came home."

"Those are complicated implications."

"Yes."

"It's uncanny. Why, society invests within you females the properties of procreation — it's a proven fact, and yet, you refuse to accept it; you don't even have pangs about giving up the little thing inside you."

"Why should I?"

"Oh, you're thinking of the source. The baby symbolizes the love of husband or lover."

"I don't understand you. I loved him who gave me this baby, but that doesn't mean I must love a baby which will hold me back."

"And of course, the man left you?"

"He was one of those pimps you were talking about. He didn't leave me intentionally. They put him in jail."

Betty rubbed her fingers together gently. She uncrossed her knees and pulled both legs together. Her feet on the floor, the doctor saw her as a little girl again.

"Momma would marry you if she could have my baby. She even promised to give up the House."

Doctor Rider knew Betty was right. He had slept more than once with the matron of the whore house. He had never considered marrying her.

"Betty, I'm not averse to marrying a prostitute, excuse me, that's what your mother is, or was, and you know it now."

"Yes I know."

"But I would never marry that pig-headed, selfish, inconsiderate tigress," the doctor continued. "She'd chew me up and spit me to my animals. The truth of the matter, Betty, is that I enjoy this so-called freedom, but this is about me. We must think about you."

"I've nothing to make you think, doctor. I want you to keep my baby. I want to go back to work. I want to leave here. What's there to think about? You think too much!"

Doctor Rider held a five by eight white card on his lap. He studied it before answering.

"Yes, I do think too much. Take Helena for example. She doesn't think, doesn't reason. What she wants she merely takes."

"Who's Helena?"

"A lioness. I've had to remove her claws. She's an advertising gimmick for the bank. Nice girl, when she's without claws, but awfully cruel with them."

"And I'm like her?"

"No, not at all. In many ways you are. But Helena welcomes a family, at least, a baby."

"Ha! I'm not like your Helena then. I don't want a baby. So you see, I'm better than an animal."

Doctor Rider threw the card onto the desk and began picking his nose. "Have you told your mother that you want to leave?"

"That's why she keeps the door locked." Betty became more confident now that the doctor had discontinued the lengthy speech. "She won't let me leave. I will though, like I've come here today."

Doctor Rider was on his feet. "You must accept it. You must! You must!"

"I won't! I'll give it to an orphanage if you don't take it. I'm too young for a baby, but I won't have an abortion. I just won't take it. I can't give it love. You see, doctor, I don't know what love is and I don't care to know because love did that to Momma and love brings those men to me. I don't want it."

Doctor Rider pretended to study the cages. "Betty, I just can't give you an answer right now."

"You want to talk to Momma?"

"Yes, she must know. Maybe we can work something out."

"I'm going to leave, doctor. That's all there is to it. I'm going to get out of this fucking town."

"Yes, I know. Come in and see Helena."

"Why?" Betty was afraid of the beast in the cage. The gray-haired man with his fatherly gestures made her rise.

"You two are alike."

"I don't like her."

"That's not fair. You've never met her."

They stared at Helena and the beast stared back, watching,

waiting for a sign of movement before she knew they were there, then fixing her searching eyes on them. She pawed the cage with her white bandages. Betty felt sorrow for the beast.

"Here's my phone number." He handed her a card. "Please call in the morning."

The veterinarian shook his head looking at Helena and Betty left.

The spring rains came that night to Clay Town. Betty read, her knees tucked under her at her mother's home. Flames from the gas grate dried the dampness from her body. The book in her lap, the Bible, dried her mental tears. She was happy. She sipped coffee and read into the early morning, not knowing why or what she read but happy with the words. Her mother was staying at the House and Betty felt happy that she was alone, sitting in front of the fire streaked grate.

Doctor Rider was unhappy talking to his animals. Helena had fallen asleep and he moved on to the dogs and cats, frightened, restless, howling beasts of domestication. They made him talk of past sins and nights of squalor. From his talk emerged the passion of want, but he was confused. He wanted Doris Gray, he wanted Betty Gray. He wanted the baby to fondle, but he did not know how to fondle. He had fostered thoughts before this, alone with his animals. Tonight, this morning, he loved words. They came to him and his animals. They were beautiful hanging unseen between the walls. Betty was a mere child, but he wanted a child to fulfill his empty passion. The hardness of the matron was disgusting. Betty was youth and he could give her more youth by giving her youth inside her stomach; signing himself to her child; giving it a birth within the womb, bringing it alive while it was alive. It was near three o'clock when Doctor Rider knocked on Mrs. Gray's door. His beard, unkempt from passing time, was white and rough when he rubbed his chin. Betty was standing before him in her night gown, the Bible resting in her grasp.

"I wanted to talk to your mother." It was a lie.

"She's at the House."

"Then I want to talk to you."

"Come in."

The flames came up to meet him as they entered the living room. He stopped, stared, felt the heat then turned to Betty. "I'll take your baby."

"Thank you." She did not move. She did not drop the Bible.

"But I want to make it mine. Do you understand?"

"Yes." She threw the Bible onto the chair and walked into the bedroom. The doctor followed her.

The Parade

It was the day before the parade and the steel presses pounding pipe, coughed throughout Clay Town. Jinny Pin watched
from the window of her office, leaning on the rotten window sill,
watching the morning grow into people. (Come, come, the sun,
the moon, the revolving earth. Come, come, my body awaits
you! Come, I am ready.) She watched Dag Mercer walk along
Grant Street on his way to the sewer pipe factory. Jinny knew
that he was in search of a job there. Dag's yearly trial for a job
was a tradition with Clay Town people. Each year, on the day
before the Clay Town Parade, Dag started for his favorite factory
with renewed intentions of finding a job. (The machine vibrates
onward until stopped by rust.) Jinny felt her breasts, big with
life, heave under her blouse, under the elastic supporters holding
them in a feminine mold, and she was happy. She sprang, legs
sprawling across the floor as the telephone rang.

"Miss Pin, if you please?"

"Harry!"

"And how's the lass this morning?"

"You're up so early. I'm glad." Jinny brushed her hair. "Come
over right away. I just got in."

"That I'll do in two shakes! Mail can wait!"

There was nothing more to say. She replaced the heavy black
phone, smiled then read another ten pages until there was noise
below. She looked up to see Harry O'Brien was standing before

196

her, the leather bag displaying edges of white and yellow envelopes, his hand filled with more white envelopes. Jinny jumped from the desk with a burst of excitement.

"You startled me Harry."

"Sure 'nuff, your mother's acting queer this morning. Didn't want to take the mail. She sent me to you."

Jinny held the bundle of letters, not caring what they contained, caring only for the morning. But Harry just stood before her, calling her to reality. "Yes, mother hasn't been feeling well lately."

"Ask me, I think she needs to sell this store." Jinny looked up and Harry changed his mind. "Well, it does keep you people busy."

Jinny remembered, 'Travaillons sans raisonner, C'est le seul moyen de rendre la via supportable.'

"Yes, and I think someday business will improve." Jinny wanted to change the conversation. "How are the children, Harry?"

"Fine. Gettin' inta all kinds of trouble like kids 're supposed to do."

"Was it very hard for Mary to carry them?" Jinny asked.

"No, not really. 'Course we lost one, you know that. They're the ones you remember the most."

Jinny became frightened. Harry, looking into her wide eyes, went on. "But you know, birth is really not birth 'cause you have the feeling they've been born somewhere before and this is just a sort of growing up place."

Jinny knew what Harry meant even if he did not. "Yes. Yes, precisely. Birth is the contribution of the universal cycle. It's only one segment they achieve here."

Again Harry felt embarrassed because he could feel it but could not understand. So he hit the desk with his hand. "You'd never know it by them kids. They're forever tearing up things. This is the third new sack I got this year."

Jinny did not want to waste words so she walked to the window and stared as if in a trance. After a chasm of silence Harry left, shaking his head and trying to understand the odd woman at the window.

Standing at the window, Jinny watched Paul Steiner, dressed in a light-weight suit, taking leave with the people he met, shaking hands, waving into shops, while Mrs. Steiner walked beside him, her head bent as if in prayer.

Perched high on a cliff, Grover MacFadden chewed on the rag weed and watched Dag Mercer bounce along below. Dag was happy. Grover and Mary watched from above, following the road through the deep cut as it reached out into other soft rolling hills with Clay Plant #3 and the Grimes' Slaughter house in easy sight of the couple stretched out above. Grover looked over the deep embankment at the retard, balancing the hamster on his shoulder.

Grover chewed the rag weed and felt empty. Phallic love had come and gone and the boy was anxious to leave as most lovers are after a prolonged chase, but Grover's thinly clad body bathing in the sweetness of sun and suspended by weeds was warm and lazy. So Grover stared at the retard, allowing the sun to seep into his body and tried to forget the phallic exhaustion.

Mary Durance squirmed against him, not wanting Grover to forget her in this pool of aftermath. Now she wanted to be loved with a different love. She also knew shame and the embarrassment made her love silent.

"Look at Dag," Grover mumbled, jealous of the half wit's freedom.

"Walking in the middle of the road and doesn't even care. Let's throw a rock at 'im and wake 'im up."

"No Grover, don't. He's not hurting you."

Grover reached for a rock in defiance of Mary's request, but in the tall grass at the edge of the cliff, missiles were not to be found. Finally he gave up and allowed his body to absorb the sun once more. Dag Mercer passed through the cut singing and balancing the hamster. The fury knob, as though understanding his incoherent words, ran from one end of Dag's shoulder to the other in spastic jerks. The anger left Grover and he laughed. Mary wiggled closer and also laughed. They watched as Dag walked along the road, crossed into a field and disappeared behind the clay stacks and kilns of the sewer pipe factory.

"Where'd he come from?" Dag had excited Grover's imagination and since it was no effort to speak, he mumbled to Mary without turning.

"From town."

"No, I mean who're his parents? He ain't got nobody now, but he must have had once? I heard his parents left him and went onto the city."

"That's not right." The warm sun made Grover feel that all things must be right. The exhaustion he felt made him realize, for the first time, that everything wasn't the way it should be.

"His father hit him in the head with a poker when he was a baby. That's why he's like that." Mary felt the importance of knowing Dag's misfortunes since her father had hired Jay Mercer, his father, in their grocery store long ago. Mr. Durance never became tired of telling about the worthlessness of Jay, and the story, through time, became exaggerated as most everything did in Clay Town.

"Boy, would I like to git hold of 'im." Grover felt anger toward the cruel father not knowing why except the presence of Dag made the world out of order.

"I'd show 'im a thing or two."

"Dag's good though. He doesn't bother anyone."

Dag Mercer had caught Mary when she fell from her first two wheel bicycle. The girl had never forgotten his gentleness. Later, when her friends in Clay Town High laughed and joked at Dag from their cars, Mary became silent. Although Dag laughed with them, she felt sorry for him. She had supplied Dag with hamster feed all though the last two years.

Suddenly she was glad Grover saw with her that everything was not right, that misery and meanness existed. She had the silly opinion that if he saw all that, he would never be cruel to her.

"I threw stones at 'im when I was a kid."

Mary shaded her eyes and felt her happiness and trust slip over the cliff.

"But I was just a kid," Grover continued to chew the rag weed. "And I didn't know no better. Funny, we grow older and he just stays the same."

Mary's heart quickened. "Growing older?"

"Sure, ain't we growing older?"

Grover lowered his voice and both he and Mary Durance knew they had tingled with the climax of childhood, and, like a seasoned soldier, stood exhausted but happy that the trial was over, and that it had been won, or, at least, partially.

Grover scrambled to his feet against the warmth of the sun, against the laziness inherent in his feelings, and she accepted his hand, coming gracefully out of the weeds as if she were a weed herself, sprouting, clinging, perfuming the air with a natural milk of earth.

They walked away from the cliff, cutting across a valley and entering the town from the hills. Grover awkwardly seized her hand and wondered what it would be like in the years ahead.

That afternoon Dag hurried to the train station, hurrying and not knowing why he ran. A determined countenance hung on his long face. Dag smiled, passing and re-passing people as though a heavenly chain of beings passed him on a platform in the nothingness of universe. He spoke to everyone, not knowing them all but speaking just the same. Yet he did not know why his steps carried him toward the lonely station after a hurried meal, unless it was for the sky bar they had demanded last summer at the factory to prove himself capable. His sprawling legs turned the corner near the Brown Hotel and he saw the hot black train hunched together in passenger cars. He knew it was the last train of the day since the railroad also proclaimed the uselessness of Clay Town. Dag passed among those who were about to board the panting vehicle. Surprised, Dag searched their eyes for understanding, but only their talk told him that they wanted to leave, not wanting to hesitate before the last scene the town offered, in front of the dilapidated depot. Dag stopped near Dody Blake and listened for a moment to the lecture from the General on military life. Dag rushed on blindly, seeking out the train master he knew must have the tool. Paul Steiner, dressed in a new suit, comforted his mother. His youthful, almost baby-face kept jerking toward the train as if he might miss it. Mrs. Steiner wept. Dag wondered why a grown woman must cry for nothing. He stumbled forward.

"Har, Paul! You go 'way?"

Paul turned to Dag, happy to divert his sorrow and happiness at leaving.

"Yes. Going east to join with a big union."

Dag was puzzled that Paul Steiner must leave. "Har, you come back?"

Paul looked at his mother then at Dag. "Maybe. I've got

to see what they have to offer." Then he changed his manhood pride for the sake of her, standing beside him. "Of course I'll be back often. The way travel is now-a-days, a guy gets around a lot. It's not like I'm going to the North Pole. Like Dody down there's going to boot camp and he'll be coming back after." Paul pointed toward his friend who was standing with the General. "I'll be back. I won't be that far away."

Mrs. Steiner spoke now that her son must leave but not wanting him to leave. "Be careful. They may treat you badly. If they do, you just come home. Now don't forget the lunch."

A hundred assurances poured from her soul and she stuttered them, staccato, the soul not knowing how to express itself in such a vulgar language of every day phrases. Paul's soul wanted to stay but he jerked it aboard, standing with one foot on the first step.

Dag stumbled forward, found the station-master, discovered that he did not own or know that the sky bar existed, in fact, he told Dag softly, rubbing his rough chin, that the tool did not exist and that someone was pulling Dag's leg.

Dag left the station as the train pulled its caterpillar-like wheels forward. Across the street, he passed Betty Gray, holding a bus ticket. He knew it to be a ticket since she had just walked out of the Brown Hotel where bus tickets were sold. Now she stared blankly at the oblong green thin cardboard. Dag stopped before the joyfully dressed girl and almost looked over her shoulder. Mousie came out of his pocket and squirmed in his hand.

"Har, Miss Gray, look at Mousie. You like Mousie?"

Betty jumped, then, turning, recognized the sorrowful smile of Dag. Once, when her baby was beginning to grow inside, she had walked, wanting to escape into death. She saw Dag sitting on the bridge and there, she met Mousie, even held the hamster. The fury animal seemed to live just for the slow-witted youth. Betty turned home that day, knowing that the animal kicking inside would somehow be like the jumping fur in Dag's hands.

Dag allowed Betty to take Mousie into her tiny hands. She held the fur against her cheek then kissed Mousie's nose.

"Har, you go away too?"

"Yes Dag. I'm going far away."

"You take baby there too?" He pointed at the protrusion which Betty began to believe beautiful.

"The baby will return."

"But you not gonna come back?"

"No. I must work to help the baby. You'll be good to Mousie, won't you?"

Dag nodded. He wished he had not met these people leaving. Inside he felt a dull space and became sick knowing they would never return. Something had happened today. He felt alone even if he had met all these friends briefly each day. They would never be there again.

That night, in his shanty in the woods near plant #3, Dag tucked Mousie in the cage then opened a bottom drawer of the old dresser and removed the Uncle Sam uniform. Worn and frayed, it had been a gift from Mr. McBridy. Dag felt honored each year to head the parade wearing it. He wanted to wear it more often during the year, but they stared with frowning faces so Dag climbed carefully into the suit, only on the day of the parade. Tonight, looking at his uniform, Dag forgot about those friends who had left. He forgot his failure to secure a job at the clay plant. He spoke rapid phrases which pleased Mousie, making her scurry around in the cage.

The next morning Dag proudly became Uncle Sam and started off toward town carrying Mousie in a velvet-lined cage. She had chewed it during the first parade, but after a repair and reprimand by Dag, she behaved herself thereafter.

Dag danced along, people laughed, and Dag was happy. He

wanted people to laugh. He tried to sing out. No words came to him so he hummed. Mousie was standing inside her cage, almost knowing the long line of people awaited their leadership.

Dr. Rider shuffled through the five by eight cards from his file. But he did not read them. Below the office on the second floor, the street came alive with the milling of people. They, like the veterinarian, awaited the parade, pretending occupation in talking, studying store windows, promising promises, just to pass time, but secretly, their eyes glanced along Grant Street and their ears were cocked for the slightest sound of drums announcing the start of the clay parade.

Dr. Rider came to a blank card, studied it, began to thumb past, but suddenly, recovering his work, plucked it from the pile. He walked to the window and studied the street for preliminary signs of the parade. He laughed at his own childish anxiety and returned to the battered desk. Why must he be caught up in these clay men's honor each year? He had no right to enjoy their parade as he had no right to enjoy their town, coming as a stranger from another country, another state, and settling here without purpose, escaping into their lives so to speak, and they knew him as a city dweller knows a bus driver or a mechanic, for he was a tool, an efficient person machine at their disposal. He had never wanted to be anything more. Only on the night of the annual parade did he mingle among them as a bitch dog longs for male company. Only on the parade night did he want to belong. Dr. Rider, being a philosopher by chosen trade and merely a veterinarian to warm his feet and feed his stomach and bring him the standards awarded to Americans, he tried to philosophize why a parade made him lonely. Putting the blank card in front of him, he scribbled on it. First it was a doodle then words appeared beside the curbed lines. Flat, ordinary letters making words they heard each day. Words were life to a philosopher - LOVE, SHARE, ALONE, FREE, LOVELY, HATE, ANOTHER, HURT, SORROW, ALIVE, CARE, JOY, SILENCE, DEATH.

As he wrote and thought how utterly non-eventful the year had been, the streets below became a world, then a universe. Dr. Rider, putting aside his pencil, studied the words and then knew inside that this last year and each year before it, unto the eons of time, and each day of that year was meaningful when considered in the light of these exact words. He had wanted to write — prosperity, security, vanity — but they did not fit on the little white card. He had scribbled too large. Presently Betty came in. The doctor, feeling the vitality of the words, made her take a seat. Over the howl of the caged animals, over the distant beating of the Clay Town High drums, he told her his revelation, or rather, he attempted to tell his youthful mistress the secret.

"In the beginning was nothing. Black has the opposite, white, and nothing must have the opposite, something so that something was a concept, or word if you like, and that word, out of nothing or blackness, which means nothing, became white, and the two struggled and from their struggle was created all. Now we came from that nothing and the concept, or the white and black struggle, was in us and made us like the beginning. It's within us but not here, or here." Dr. Rider touched his body and Betty stared in hypnotic wonderment.

"Nor here, but deep inside us. So each is born from this nothingness and becomes part of the struggle, but the struggle has been complicated by the concept which has been confused in the very struggle." He broke the pencil, the pause was shattered by the sound of an explosion. Dr. Rider rushed to the window in time to see a black puff of smoky cloud in the sky. An aerial firework had been discharged from the stadium where the evening festivities were being prepared. He turned to Betty who had joined him at the window. "Bad omen," he philosophized. "Those aerial bombs shouldn't be exploded until later."

Betty felt more secure now that Dr. Rider had left his sanctimonious speeches. "No. They're announcing the start of the parade. Here it comes!"

Dr. Rider stared out the window. "Bad omen nonetheless." His hand rested so that her breasts heaved beneath his fingers. He knew that he could contemplate the secret of life, but here, beneath his fingers, she felt the origin. He was happy to hold her. The seeds of skepticism, which Clay Town residents call insanity, and their physicians, coming from great schools of the country, call manic depressive, had taken germ in Dr. Rider long ago.

The parade, to him, seemed a star out of the universe which describes the whole. Six hours later Dr. Rider would be dead, a heart attack or was it a result of a subject who had dived to the bottom of thought, taken hold of its fiery firmament and couldn't carry it without scourging himself.

Betty had purchased the ticket to Columbus even though she loved Dr. Rider. She did not stay for the funeral, hating the smell of death and flowers.

The parade passed below. To the important man from Cleveland, a guest of Mr. Golding, it was a ridiculous spectacle, people driving decorated floats, looking like replicas of sewer pipe plants; the gold and black uniformed players were off key in the Clay Town High band, and the time spent on Grant Street watching such foolishness was long and tedious. The fat industrialist from Cleveland had not felt the sparks of the universe gaily dancing around him — how could he, these were not his kind of people — Dr. Rider, watching from the second story building thought them people of all times. Gay, happy crowds made up of lonely, sorrowful, striving individuals. Dr. Rider knew that passions poured past, in harmony with the discordant music, flowing along against the out of step rhythm of the people, clashing and making life move below him. Dr. Rider knew, obscure, small forgotten and escaping, what the fat industrialist did not know, that the parade lived in the hearts of the people and was part of the people because it allowed them to rush onto the street, sweep the mechanical cars out of their path and walk free and proud and unburdened in the coolness of night.

It happened as the main import of the wiggling parade passed in front of the Westway. The bright colors had made the people intoxicated. It was the renaissance dancing against the destructive elements of science, red cars, red fire trucks, purple and pink dresses blowing in a slight breeze, gold and black uniforms, led by silver white hot dresses kissing the bare, pink knees of majorettes, florescent orange signs staring into the crowds; it was the renaissance of America in a dying clayish tradition.

The General had been swept along in the intoxication, but his sorrow needed the stimulant of whiskey to raise his spirits. So the General got drunk long before he mounted the steed which would carry him high above the others along Grant Street and later into the ballpark for the crowning of the queen and best floats. In front of the Westway the horse bolted and the General, intoxicated, fell far to the ground. The horse, excited by the screaming crowd, ran from his downed rider. The crowd did not try to stop the horse. Some gathered around the unconscious man, and soon the sound of an ambulance cut the night air.

After the parade resumed with dampened energy, Dag watched Mr. McBridy drive the screaming ambulance into the distance. The siren was unnecessary, but Mr. McBridy, feeling his importance, screamed through the crowd, sending the people onto the sidewalk.

The gaily dressed Uncle Sam cried as he led the parade. Mousie, excited by the accident, began chewing the velvet-lined cage.

They entered the stadium. There was a cheer from those who had gathered in the stands to watch. The floats continued to drive around the cinder track. The judges bowed their heads and made marks on pads as the floats passed. The people in the stands cheered their favorites.

Karl Schmidt, the mayor, acted as an honorary judge. His wife, Alice, and her father, were two of the real judges.

In the stands, Jinny Pin sat with her mother. They did not cheer. Harry O'Brien stared at Jinny from several rows back.

Jimmy and Dorothy Wilson sat on a top row bench, away from the cheering crowd.

Grover MacFadden and Mary Durance were more conspicuous. They too held hands, but they released their bondage as Plant #3's float passed. They both clapped for Grover's local entry.

Dag's moments of glory were ended for another year. In the infield, Dag walked toward the area where the fireworks were set up. He passed Larry and Jimmy McBridy, who were waiting for the ambulance to return. "Har. Jimmy see parade? See Dag lead?"

"Sure did Dag! You were great," Jimmy answered. "Great! Great! Great!"

"Dag and Mousie lead way."

"Your costume's torn, Dag," Larry shouted pointing toward the stripes of the Uncle Sam jacket.

Dag inspected the material and discovered the large rip at the shoulder. He peeled the material and stared at the exposed shirt not knowing what to say.

"Better have it fixed or they won't allow you to lead next year's parade!" Larry laughed.

"Uncle Sam come apart, har." Dag hurried on not wishing to continue the discourse. He replaced the material and patted it. His efforts at cosmetic repair came undone. He walked toward the roped-off area where the fireworks stood with scarecrow resemblance. The Uncle Sam shoulder material flapped with each awkward step.

Dag knew Jim Handley from past events. Once he was allowed to help with setting up the missiles until Dag knocked over several displays.

"Har. Mr. Handle. Dag give signal to go boom!" Dag jumped into the air to emphasize the explosion.

"Hi kid. My name's Handley. Jim Handley. You can give the signal from way over there if you call me by my right name." Jim pointed toward the stands a safe distance away.

"Har. Jim Hardley. Dagburt Mercer help."

"Tell you what, Dagburt. You watch that truck up there by the gate and I'll pay you a dollar."

"Watch truck?" Dag asked looking in the direction where Jim pointed.

"Yeah. It's filled with another display. I'm headed over to a town near Pittsburgh. Got another fireworks on Sunday."

"Har. Dag watch truck good. Don't let nobody smoke around it. No smoke. Mousie and Dag watch."

Jim handed Dag a dollar and returned to his last minute inspection. Dag started toward the distant panel truck. The judging of the floats had ended. The mayor and the other judges were tabulating votes. A one hundred dollar prize would be awarded the best entry.

Many from the bleachers were lined up at the hot dog stand

located in the infield. One of the floats had parked next to the fireworks truck. Dag sauntered forward to inspect the intruder to his guarding space.

The float represented the daughters of the pioneers and, although elaborately constructed, it stood little chance of winning. The daughters of the pioneers were not popular with the mayor since their attempt to oust him from office.

Dag grunted approval and climbed onto the flatbed truck. There was a rustic table, two old chairs, and several replicas of old clay mining machinery. Dag inspected the pick and shovel then sat down, placing the velvet-lined Mousie cage on the table. He noticed a kerosene lamp hanging on the makeshift wooden wall which separated the cab of the truck from the display. "Har. No smoke," he whispered to Mousie.

Dag rose and attempted to take the lantern from its hook. It burned dimly. He succeeded in removing the lantern but could not open it. He blew on the globe several times without extinguishing the flame. Attempting to raise the globe he knocked the lantern off the table. Mousie ran frantically around the velvet cage and managed to squeeze out through the hole chewed during the parade.

Dag had started for the lantern, which was spilling kerosene. He spied Mousie's escape and hesitated, not knowing what to do.

The lantern on the ground beside the float erupted in flames. Crepe paper decorating the sides of the float caught on fire. Instead of retrieving the lantern or Mousie, Dag ran to a nearby water fountain and filled a discarded plastic cup he found on the ground.

"Mousie! Come back!" he shouted as he returned to the fire which burned around the gasoline tank of the float.

Dag threw the cup of water into the flames and returned for more. As he was filling the cup he spied Mousie dart beneath the fireworks truck. He did not leave his post and waited for the cup to fill.

Jimmy McBridy spied the fire from the infield as they greeted the ambulance. "There's a fire!" he shouted. Jimmy started to run toward the vehicles but it was too late. The gasoline tank exploded. The resulting force knocked Jimmy to the ground. Through the flames he saw Dag attempting to push the fireworks truck. It was on fire.

Larry picked Jimmy up just as the second truck exploded with volcanic intensity. Sparkling missiles flared across the infield. Their fiery rooster-tails gave the effect of burning water flooding the stadium. Streaks of errant projectiles cascaded into the stands spreading fiery stars among the gathering. Shrill whistling sounds followed by explosions from the volatile rockets were punctuated by human screams as the stadium became an erupting volcanic caldera.

The three McBridys crawled beneath the ambulance. Jimmy watched the rockets explode around him, and knew the fear of war.

The unexpected rocket assault ended in a matter of minutes. Latent bombs continued to explode erratically as the people fled the stadium, jumping fences, ducking into doorways, driving floats across the infield and through the gates to safety of the outside.

Dag was among the casualties. No one gave much thought to Mousie. There would be no monuments built to Dag, who remained by his job, attempting to save lives. Charred pieces of the Uncle Sam uniform were buried with him. Reverend Rosewood did not praise his frantic attempt to overcome adversity. He merely recited the valley psalm and asked the Lord to receive this newly departed brethren.

But then, heroes are made by people, not events.

It was the summer of 1954. The cycle had ended.

After the burial the people returned to work in the few remaining sewer pipe plants surrounding the town.

They would all disappear with time...

About The Author

An award winning poet, short story writer and documentarian, the author has written, produced, and directed over 200 film/video productions, many focusing on current events, social issues, historical, and international subjects. An English major graduate of The Ohio State University, he became a writer-producer while at WOSU-TV, moved to WITF-TV, Hershey, PA, then to Washington, D.C. working at WRC/NBC-TV. In Los Angeles and Tucson he is working on another anthology, "The Bizarre Shop," a video series, "On These Ruins," about ancient archeological sites, and as a freelance writer-director. He married his wife, Ada, while attending Ohio State.